*The Museum of
Shadows & Reflections*

Stories

The Museum of SHADOWS & REFLECTIONS

STORIES
BY CLAIRE DEAN
With illustrations by Laura Rae

Unsettling Wonder : 2016

'Raven' © 2010, *Scheherezade's Bequest* 10, Cabinet des Fées*
'Feather Girls' © 2010, *The Adirondack Review*, Volume XI, no. 2*
'A Book Tale' © 2010, *Flax027*, Litfest*
'The Silent Kingdom' © 2008, *New Fairy Tales* 1*
'Growing Cities' © 2011, *The Pygmy Giant**
'Glass, Bricks, Dust' © 2013, *New Fairy Tales: Essays and Stories, Unlocking Press**
'The Sand Ship' © 2011, *a Capella Zoo* 7*
'Moth Light' © 2013, *Magpie Magazine**
'Marionettes' © 2011, first published as a Nightjar Press chapbook*
'Stone Sea' © 2012, *Metazen**
'Chorden-under-Water' © 2011, the Oxfam Books Blog*
'Casting Ammonites' © 2013, *Shadows and Tall Trees* 5*
'The Woman Who Wore Frost Slippers' © 2013, *Unsettling Wonder*
* originally published under the surname Massey

The Museum of Shadows and Reflections
Copyright © 2016 Claire Dean. All Rights Reserved Worldwide.
ISBN 978-1-907881-49-7 HB
ISBN 978-1-907881-61-9 PB
A catalogue for this title is available from the British Library.
10 9 8 7 6 5 4 3 2 1

*Claire Dean has asserted her moral right
to be identified as the author of this work.*

Except in the case of quotations embedded in critical articles or reviews, no part of this book may be reproduced or transmitted in any form or by any means, electronic or mechanical, including photocopying, recording, or by any information storage and retrieval system, without permission in writing from the publisher.

First published in 2016 by Unsettling Wonder,
an imprint of Papaveria Press.
Papaveria is a Circle Six company.
www.unsettlingwonder.com

Typeset in Arno Pro 12 by 14
Printed in the United Kingdom

Contents

Part 1: Shadows

Raven	3
Feather Girls	9
A Book Tale	17
The Silent Kingdom	29
Growing Cities	35
Glass, Bricks, Dust	39
The Museum of Shadows and Reflections	47

Part 2: Reflections

The Sand Ship	61
Moth Light	69
Stone Sea	75
Marionettes	81
Chorden-under-Water	93
Casting Ammonites	101
The Woman Who Wore Frost Slippers	107

For George and Sam, always.

*In loving memory of
Florence Dean
1923-2015*

*New myths spring up
beneath each step we take.*

SHADOWS

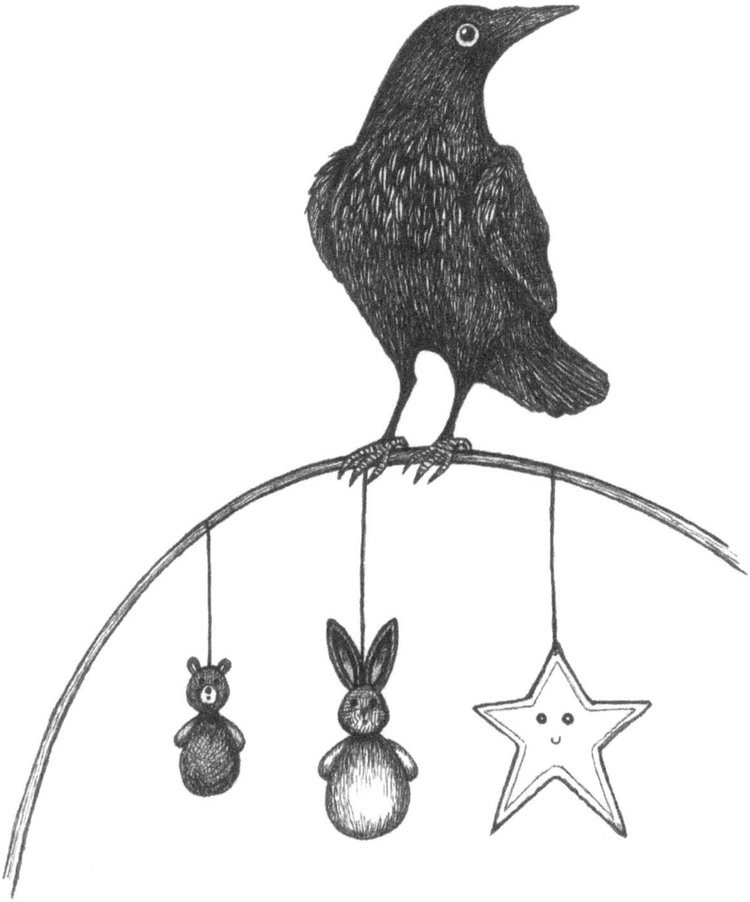

Raven

> There was once a queen and she had a little daughter, who was as yet a babe in arms; and once the child was so restless that the mother could get no peace, do what she would; so she lost patience, and seeing a flight of ravens pass over the castle she opened the window and said to her child, 'Oh, that thou wert a raven and couldst fly away, that I might be at peace.'

SHE CHANGED ALMOST IMMEDIATELY, SPRANG FROM my arms into the living room window, clattered at the glass with beak and claws as she tried desperately to make her wings work.

I watched her watch the flock of ravens as they flew out of sight, over the terraced roofs, chasing wind torn scrags of cloud. I was still holding my arms as though to cradle her and support her head. She shifted on the windowsill, tried to extend her wings and began to cry. Not the shrieking mewl that had been piercing me for weeks but a raw caw-cawing sound.

I sat down on the floor. She perched on the edge of the windowsill, claws digging into the paintwork, and turned to face me, head cocked to one side, her blue eyes darker, black feathers shining in the thin winter sunlight. She clicked her beak. I wondered if I should shut the window in case she tried to fly again, but she didn't move. Neither did I.

I looked at the washing basket on the floor beneath the window, heaped with clean babygros, blankets, and sheets that needed sorting and putting away. In the corner of the room was the moses basket I tried to get her to sleep in during the day. I knew an unsucked dummy lay on the yellow sheet, beside the place where her head should have been.

She clicked her beak again, then stretched her wings. Already so big—surely she should have become a baby raven. Or was this what baby ravens looked like?

We each sat and watched the other. It was starting to get dark. I should have put the lamp on, but I didn't move. She was quiet now. The streetlights snapped on outside and her feathers looked even blacker against their orange glow. I couldn't see her eyes. Tony would be home soon. I didn't know what he was going to say.

She shifted from foot to foot and then stretched her wings again. She jumped a little. She was going to try to fly. I imagined her crashing towards me. Her beak aimed at my eyes. I clenched them shut. There was a clatter. I opened them and for a moment I had no sense of where she was in the room. I looked at the empty windowsill and up at the open window. Then I heard her beak clicking. She was perched on top of the baby gym. I'd told Tony that she didn't need it up yet, still too young, it was just clutter. He'd put it up anyway.

She gripped the orange plastic and experimented with bobbing her head down till she could bat the assortment of jingling animals. As she got more confident she managed to knock a button on one and a grating, echoey version of 'Twinkle Twinkle' began to play. She paused to listen, then knocked the button again.

I shifted my weight to get up. She didn't notice. She was too preoccupied with her toy. My legs had gone numb. I struggled to stand and gripped the settee as I waited for the pins and needles to prickle through them. I stumbled to the lamp and switched it on. It made her jump. She landed on the floor and stared up at me. Started to click her beak again.

I wondered if she might be hungry. I didn't know what ravens ate. All we had in was a freezer full of microwave meals and a packet of Jammie Dodgers. I went to get her a Jammie Dodger. I took longer over opening the biscuit tin than I should have. It was brighter in the kitchen. I knew she hadn't flown out of the window. I could still hear 'Twinkle Twinkle' grating on and on.

I took the biscuit in to her and put it on the floor, as close as I dared get. She jumped down, nudged it with her beak, looked at me, went back to the biscuit, pushed it a little way across the carpet then looked at me again. She cawed. She hopped towards me. She was looking at my chest.

I started to get the idea. I'd always said there was no way I was breastfeeding her once she got teeth. I hadn't expected a beak. I shook my head and backed away towards the door, back towards the brightness of the kitchen light. She cawed again. I remembered the breast pump that was still in its packaging on top of the freezer. It had looked too fiddly. I'd been too tired to work out how to use it. The box said you had to sterilise every part of it, and we hadn't bought a steriliser because I was breastfeeding.

She cawed again. I went to get the box.

Back on the settee, I tore off the plastic wrapping and pulled the various implements out. We'd have to do without sterilising. A raven was different to a baby anyway. I followed the instructions to construct it. In the 'Top Tips' it said you had to relax to be able to express milk. She cawed and hopped to my feet. I held one arm out so I could bat her away if she launched at me. She cried and it sounded more like her old cry. I pulled my swollen left breast from my bra and milk began to spray out, doing half the job for me. I attached the sucker end and began to pump the handle. It hurt. I watched her watching me.

I couldn't give it to her in the bottle that I'd pumped it into. I went to get a saucer. Her claws scrabbled on the laminate dining room floor behind me. I didn't look down, just went straight back into the living room and placed the saucer of thin off-white milk on the floor. She dipped her beak into it and extended her thin black tongue. She made a strange rattling noise as she drank.

Sated, she burped. Something I'd never been able to get her to do after a feed. She stretched her wings one last time before curling them back into herself.

She was a baby lying on her rug when Tony came in. 'Great,' he said, looking at the packaging on the settee, 'you managed to figure out the pump.'

She's three now. Bright and troubling. She hides things, steals things, eats worms. People tell me all three-year-olds do those things, but do they?

Her eyes have changed from greyish blue to brown. In the morning I find black feathers on her pillow amongst the fine blonde hairs she's shed in the night.

But we play, and the days go quicker than they did. Most days I don't worry about her too much until we get to the playground. I see her at the top of the climbing frame—arms outstretched—and I wonder how long it will be before she tries to fly.

Feather Girls

'You have to catch their coats whilst they're young.' That was the saying he'd been brought up with, in a village full of thin, white-haired women who saw nothing wrong in telling their sons how best to trap a girl, as they themselves had once been trapped. The sun sparkled on the peat-coloured lake below, making magic of dun. He took his time on the long road down to the village. Avoided pot holes and sheep muck and loose chips of stone tumbled from the walls. Midges rolled in clouds overhead. He tugged at the long grass that sprouted at the roadside and bent it, twisted it, threaded it through his fingers, snapped it. All these years of going to meet her and yet still, every time, he felt like a lad. His stomach might as well be in a boat out on the lake.

The sign outside the Hare and Anchor was cracked, and the paint so faded you could barely make out the image of a brown hare, its ears wrapped around a silver anchor. It was a locals' pub, sandwiched between crumbling cottages with mildewed net curtains, further up the steep hill than outsiders cared to venture. Tourists were catered for beside the lake, where they swarmed off ferries into gift shops and outdoor clothing shops and took cream tea in cafés where the lacy nets were clean. She would pass all that on her way up the hill. Had she left the lake already? Crossed the narrow shingle beach, stepped on to the pavement, webbed feet becoming toes, dripping feather coat hung over what was her wing but now an arm.

'Usual, Bill?' Mary, the landlady, put aside the television listings magazine she'd been reading.

'And a glass of tap water and a—'

'Packet of salt and vinegar crisps. Meeting her tonight, are you, love?'

He didn't reply, just waited for his pint of mild to be drawn and watched the empty table by the fireplace.

'You know,' said Mary, 'you should have caught her coat whilst she was young.'

A collection of regulars cluttered the bar, all grey-haired men a similar age to him. He knew many of them had caught themselves feather girls. On summer evenings when they were lads they would gather beside the lake and try to gain favour by lobbing in the biggest pieces of bread. Home baked worked best. His cousin Johnny had walloped a whole loaf in once but that had backfired when a greedy girl near choked on it. He married her though. Eileen she took as her name.

He handed Mary the exact change and carried the drinks and crisps over to the table. It wasn't like her to be late. He placed the glasses on the already sodden beer mats and shook a dribble of mild from his fingers.

The fire wasn't lit. Mary was stingy with the coal, still too early in the year for a fire whatever the chill in the air said. Collections of one kind or another littered the pub, whisky boxes, empty wine bottles, framed pictures of 1930s' film stars who would never have visited a place like this. There were three dart boards on one wall, but nobody remembered where the darts were. On the mantelpiece there were stacks of glass ash trays, scorched and lined with grit. A monument to times past, or testament to the fact Mary could never throw anything away.

He hadn't heard her come in but there she was. The pale skin of her cheeks looked damp, her dark eyes nervous. She was tall and slight in her downy white under dress, and she compulsively twiddled her fingers, as though when she had them she couldn't bear not to be using them. She tucked her feather coat beneath the table and perched on a stool. He shifted his legs back so he wouldn't have to know the feathers were there, brushing against his trousers.

He opened the crisps, split the foil of the packet and pulled it apart so they could share.

Delicate lines appeared around her eyes and mouth as she smiled. She tried to speak but her voice was too hoarse; she dipped her head. He nodded. It always took a while for the words to come out right, for her to find her human voice. He didn't have that excuse.

She plucked at the crisps with her fingers. He always found this movement intriguing to watch; it was as though her fingers became her beak and her long thin arm took the place of her graceful neck.

As they found their voices they talked of the lake, the speed of the boats, the damaged reed beds, squabbles with her neighbours, unruly coots and forever diving cormorants, the quality of the waterwort, the spread of swamp stonecrop.

'I'll take these for you, shall I?' Mary intruded, fingers already grasping the not quite empty glasses. 'I'll bring you some more, and another packet of them crisps too.'

She nodded. She wouldn't speak to Mary, or to anyone else but him as far as he'd ever seen.

His grandmother had been a feather girl, strict and cold. She'd never found where his grandfather had hidden her coat. He'd heard people from elsewhere tell other tales about white feathers; if you found one it meant an angel had visited, or there were rumours about young girls giving them to men in civvies during the war to show them up as cowards. In the village a found feather meant one of the girls was itching to fly away. They sometimes grew back in the crook of an elbow or at the back of the neck, but they soon fell out. He had found one of his Grandmother's in the bread bin once. Stuffed it in his pocket, then kept it for weeks tucked between the pages of a precious Dandy.

Finally he'd set it out to sail on the lake, on a December day as the cloudy surface was beaten with rain.

His wife came from the south. She'd had no time for the 'silly swan stories', said the abundance of white-haired women in the village was down to inbreeding. She'd said a lot else as well. She'd flown off herself as soon as the children were grown.

Mary plonked the glasses down. Foam and water coursed from the soggy mats and pooled on the table. Mary waited for a moment, but soon gave up and stalked back to the bar.

He split the packet, as before. The tips of her fingers touched his knuckles as they both reached for a crisp. He pulled away.

He already knew how the evening would go. How the dusk would settle outside as they talked in hushed voices. How, when they had sat for too long with the empty glasses and the empty crisp packet between them they would know it was time to go. She would clutch her feather coat and they would say a quick goodbye on the doorstep of the pub, between the abandoned hanging baskets. He would try not to watch her walk down the road towards the lights that twinkled on the water at the edge of the lake. He would try not to worry about the chill in the air and her shivering because she would not put her feather coat back on until she'd reached the water. He would try not to linger on the buckled moorland road, watched by his stern-faced sheep, their coats grey in the twilight. He would try not to hear his plodding footsteps matched by the sound of wings beating overhead as he made his way towards the squat stone building that was home.

For now, he would watch her fingers peck at the last crumbs in the crisp packet, and listen to the collection of voices drone beside the bar, and the clink of glasses as Mary pretended to tidy up.

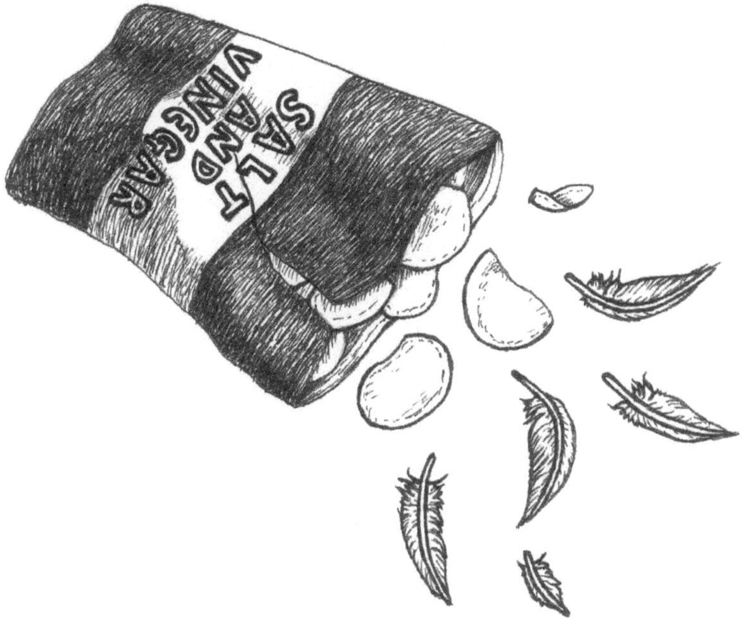
SALT
AND
VINEGAR

A Book Tale

HE WAS ALWAYS LOOKING FOR THE BOOK. IN CHARITY shops, at car boot sales, in libraries, on every shelf of every second hand bookshop he could find. He didn't know the title or who had written it. He remembered the pages were yellowed and it smelled like an old book should, but he only knew scraps of one of the stories inside it: an old fairy tale that had given him nightmares since he was six years old.

It was a Friday night. My flat smelled of the Chinese we'd finished hours before and we'd both drunk too much red wine. He tried to tell me the story again, 'It was about a boy who was locked in a cage in a forest.'

'Who put him in there?' I asked.

'I don't know.'

'Well, how did he get out?'

'I don't know.'

'Did he get out? It wasn't one of those fairy tales where the child gets eaten, was it?'

'I can't remember.'

Saturday morning, I was trying to doze but he was wide awake. He'd dreamt about the long thin fingers that held the key that locked the cage. He said he had to go out. I burrowed into the quilt. I was thinking about coffee and a bacon butty and a heap of newspapers and not getting dressed until teatime. He said he'd be back later.

That first week I rang his mobile every few minutes. I kept it up long after the phone had died. I stood for an endless trickle of days with my finger on the buzzer to his flat. There was no answer. No one in the building had seen him. We hadn't been together that long, I hadn't met his friends or family. I didn't know who else to ask.

Rain swamped the pavement in town. There was hardly anyone about. A woman was busking though, a fiddler. She stood outside the boarded-up Woolworths, and dark wet curls clung to her face as she played through the rain. She was singing too, in a clear, sweet voice. I felt sorry for her performing to an empty street but I had no money on me so didn't want to stop. Then I heard the words: 'The boy in the cage was locked from his love, and the girl set out to find him. She searched on the moor and she searched in the town and she ran through the forest to find him…'

My jaw clenched. My throat started to burn. The fiddler's long thin fingers danced faster and faster up and down the neck of the violin. I got closer and glanced into the case at her feet expecting to see a handful of coppers on the damp green velvet. But I saw hills. Everything tilted dangerously. I fell forwards, tumbling into a confusion of air and icy rain. My ears screamed with the pressure. When it stopped, I could still hear the lilt of her voice but it was coming from above. I was sitting on a hillside. Damp grass pressed beneath my fingers. The rest of the song was swept away by the wind.

I stood up. Hills surrounded me, as though I'd landed in a nest of them. I walked. First in one direction and then, when I'd got sick of the wind buffeting me, back in the other. There were no landmarks to aim for, just endless grass and grey clouds and the occasional speck of a bird swooping past. I walked until I had blisters.

'Oi!' A girl sprung out of the hillside. Her dress was as green as the moor and I'd trodden on it.

'I'm sorry,' I said, 'I didn't see you.'

'It's made of grass,' she said, 'and rain. My dress.' And she plonked herself back down. With her long thin fingers she set about weaving a strand of grass into the patch of the dress I'd damaged. Then she squinted up at the sky, plucked a string of raindrops from the air and threaded them into her bodice. 'You looking for someone?'

'Yes,' I said. 'How did you know?'

'You won't find him on the moor.'

'Is he in here? Do you know where he is? Which way should I go?'

'I think,' she said, 'you're supposed to do something for me first.' She peered up at me. 'I'm sick of looking like the hills. I want to wear clothes that the rain runs off, not through. Like yours.'

'We could swap,' I said.

The dress slid on easily enough but the grass scratched at my stomach and breasts and the damp cold of it made me shudder. 'Which way?'

'Just walk into the wind,' she said, and skipped off across the moor in my jeans and t-shirt, my jacket and trainers. She'd even taken my knickers and bra.

I walked the way I'd been going before. The grass prickled beneath my arms and raindrops worked their way loose and streamed down my legs, but I found I could cut through the wind—each barefoot step covered the distance of ten.

I thought the old lady with the handcart was a boulder. She was cloaked in a granite-coloured shawl, head bowed. But as I got closer she shuffled forwards a little and forms began to emerge from the grey bulk. Her pale, wrinkled face was tucked beneath a bonnet beneath the hood of her cloak and her crumpled shoes peeped out from underneath her tattered skirts. I crossed the distance between us in one step. She smiled. She had one yellow tooth at the bottom and one at the top. She was pulling the cart behind her. 'Now, shhh, love,' she said, 'we'll have to whisper, it's still night time in there.'

'In where?' I whispered.

She prodded the cloth-covered mound on the cart. Then she took hold of the handles again and shuffled a little further forwards.

'Can I help?' I asked.

She stopped and had a good look at me. 'No,' she said, 'you'd pull it too fast.' She set off again. I barely moved trying to stay alongside her.

'Have you lost something?' she said.

'Someone.'

'Aye, well he's probably in there.' She jabbed her thumb at the cart. 'If you help me, love, I can help you.'

'I did offer to help pull,' I said.

'I'm thinking more of material goods—trinkets, knick-knacks, treasures.'

I clutched at the skirt of wet grass. All of my clothes had gone to the girl. The only thing I had left was my watch. I took it off my wrist and held it out to her.

'What would I want with time?' She snorted and shuffled forwards again.

'Actually, it's not very good at time,' I said. 'It was my Grandma's. You have to wind it up at least three times a day and it usually runs either ten minutes fast or ten minutes slow. Or it stops altogether.'

'Well, maybe.' She stretched out her long thin fingers, snatched it, sniffed it, then tucked it beneath her cloak. 'Happen I'll make it morning now,' she said. She turned back to the cart and tugged the black cloth away.

On the back of the cart sat a miniature town. Rows of red-bricked houses ran up and down steep slopes. There were derelict mills and bricked-up warehouses, one tall chimney, a main street full of shops, most of which had displays littered with 'clearance' and 'closing down' signs. I counted seven pubs with boarded-up windows. As I stared down into the town I dug my toes into the moor, I didn't want to fall into another place.

'It's a lost town,' said the old woman. 'Not much call for it, no right place for it, so I'm taking care of it for a while. Won't be able to keep it going forever, mind.'

'Is he really in there?' I asked.

'If you've lost him, he probably is.'

I lifted my foot, trying to judge if I could climb in.

'Ey, ey, ey!' she said. 'Don't you be clambering in there with your giant muddy feet. You don't get in there that way. And you can't go in dressed like that, you look a right tuttle. Fetch me something to throw, sticks would do it, or else stones.'

As I scrabbled about in the grass she rummaged beneath her cloak and produced a book of matches. She struck one, opened a tiny mill door and thrust the flame inside. Broken windows flared and a puff of smoke erupted from the one tall chimney. Soon there was a long thin thread of it curling up into the air.

'Right, give them here.'

I handed over a collection of small pebbles and with a few casual throws she managed to hit the specks of birds out of the sky. 'Just gives them a bad head.' Then she darted about—in a way I would never have imagined she could move—and pulled and pocketed a handful of feathers from each prone lump before lobbing them back up into the sky.

'I'm making you a dress of smoke and feathers,' she said.

I drifted down to the cobbled street like a bedraggled, dirty cloud. It was a drizzly dawn. I was glad there was no one about as I tried to walk with sodden feathers clinging to my ankles. I headed for the main street, which curved slightly up a hill. As I walked I realised it was easier to let the dress carry me just a little way above the pavement. I could avoid puddles that way too.

There was a bookshop half way up. I knew he would be in there. A bell tinkled as I pushed open the door. There were no lights on inside.

'Hello?' I called out.

No answer.

He'd told me once that he always went straight for the bottom shelves in bookshops. No one wants to crouch down, or practically lie on the floor to read the spines, he'd said, so that's where all the best things get left. I crouched, conscious of the smoky smell of my dress and the wet feathers between my legs.

In the grey light, I ran my fingers along a row of dull brown spines. One book was placed the wrong way round. As I tried to pull it from the shelf a sheaf of pages came loose in my hand. I tried to stuff them back in but more paper came tumbling out, too much paper for the book. I unravelled and smoothed the cascade of pages. It was a dress. There was no sign of anyone to tell me what to do or to demand an exchange. Row after row of silent books watched me. The only sound was the delicate whir of a milk van climbing the street outside.

I stripped the smoke and feathers off and slipped the book dress on. The pages were mottled and yellowed with age. It smelled just like an old book should. There was a crumpling sound. The dress tightened round me binding me inwards and downwards. As I spiralled to the floor the bookshelves shot up until they towered above me. I knew I had to go into the book. I hitched up the rustling paper skirt, clambered on to the bottom shelf and plunged into the murky space between the front and back covers—the gap where the pages should have been. My footsteps sounded first on the wooden shelf, and then on dry leaves. Inky shadows of trees separated themselves from the darkness and I knew I was in a forest. There was no path to follow. Shadow branches scratched at my arms and snagged my hair. Soft dust fell like rain.

I found him in a cage that swung from the shadow of an old oak tree. He was curled up in his old brown duffel coat, eyes closed. He had a beard. 'Owen,' I said.

He opened his eyes, they were crusted with sleep. 'I found the book,' he said.

'How do we get out?' I rattled the cage. 'How does the story end?'

'You need to find the key before the one with the long thin fingers comes back.'

'Find it where?'

'I don't know. I can't remember.'

There were other footsteps in the darkness. I grabbed a page from the hem of the dress and read as fast as I could until I got to a sentence that said: 'She grabbed a page from the hem of her dress and read as fast as she could until she got to a sentence that said she should tear a ragged key shape from it…'

I tore a ragged key shape from the page and thrust it into the lock. The cage door swung open. I grabbed his hands.

As we ran through the forest she followed us. At times I could feel her cold breath on my neck. Her long thin fingers clawed at the dress, tearing loose page after page. These swirled about in a storm of paper before settling ahead of us into a path. Here and there, between the cracks of the pages of the path, there were feathers, and further along tufts of grass. When it started to rain the words ran into one another and smeared into a stony grey. I pulled the last scraps of the book from my stomach and crushed them into a small ball. Owen gave me his duffel coat to wear. 'I know you think it smells,' he said, 'but you can't walk home naked.'

The ink-smudged path became the chewing gum pocked slabs of the pavement outside Woolworths. There was no sign of the fiddler, but the violin case was still there. Clutching Owen's hand, I threw the ball of paper on to the damp green velvet. We watched the remains of the story scatter over the hills below.

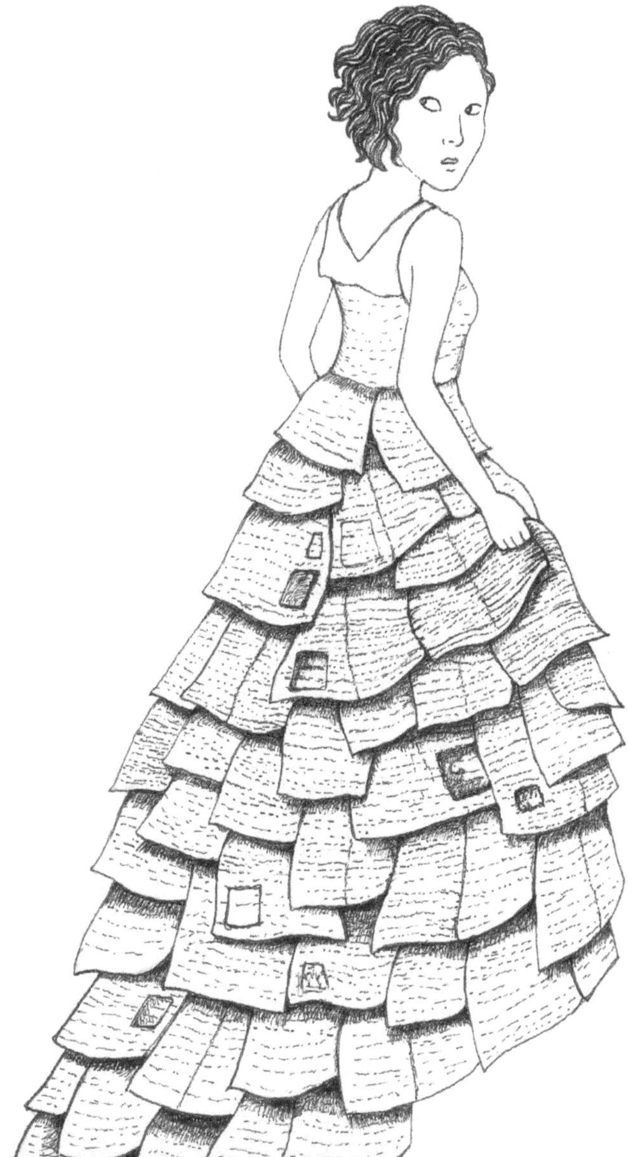

The Silent Kingdom

ONCE THERE WAS AND THERE WAS NOT A KINGDOM wrapped in silence. The streets were paved with blankets to smother the sound of footsteps, and even the horses wore satin slippers. Everyone and everything lived their lives hushed and shushed. Cooks stirred the soup without ever touching the spoon against the sides of the pan, children played in the street with gags tied tightly round their mouths, and all birds were swiftly shot with silent arrows.

This silence was born from a spell. The spell lay heavily on the old king's shoulders because he had asked for it. When his only child and heir was small, she had had the loudest voice in the kingdom, and she never stopped asking questions. From the moment she awoke to the moment she slept, the palace walls shook with 'Whys?' and 'Wheres?' and 'Whats?'

'Why are you a king, Daddy?', 'Where is the edge of the world?', 'What did cook put in the soup?'

The young princess's face was bright with curiosity as she launched from one question to the next. The Wise Men in the king's council muttered that it wouldn't do, it was inappropriate. They even whispered in the king's ear that careless questions could be dangerous. And so the king gave them permission to intervene.

The first Wise Man said they should enchant her tongue so it would not speak.

The second Wise Man said they should enchant her mind so it would not think to speak.

The third Wise Man said they should enchant her soul so it would not want to speak.

Unable to come to an agreement, they decided to try all three. They spent seventy-seven days and nights concocting the spell. They sent for arcane ingredients, they drew secret signs, they muttered forbidden words.

And they muddled it.

The princess could still speak and still thought to speak and still wanted to speak, but the moment she uttered a sound she started to crack. And not only that: every sound shook through her. More and more faint cracks appeared as the Wise Men muttered and her tears splashed to the floor.

The king sent at once for a witch who was forced to live on the shoreline at the very edge of the kingdom. The princess was hurriedly covered with the thickest blankets that could be found but still every footstep, every whisper cracked her a little more.

When the witch arrived, she dressed the girl's wounds with strips of silence and soothed her into a deep sleep so that the cracks could heal, but she could not undo the spell. The Wise Men muttered, but they had no answers. The spell could not be undone.

The old king realised how close he was to losing his only child and heir, so he outlawed sound at once. The law was written on strips of paper that were passed mutely about the kingdom: 'Not a sound will be heard in this kingdom again, by order of His Majesty the King. Hereafter, anyone who makes a sound shall be punished with immediate, silent death.'

And the kingdom fell silent. Even the wind left for places where it could bluster and shriek. Years passed, and the only sound that remained in the kingdom was the patter of falling rain, for (try as they might) the Wise Men could not banish the rainclouds. And as the princess lay on her silken bed she lifted her golden earmuffs just a little so that she could hear the rain at her window, calling her out into the world. Each drop hammered and echoed through her body until she tingled with delight, and she knew she had to escape.

The old king kept to his bed. His age and his worries were too heavy for him to carry around. And as servants fussed silently around him, the princess slipped out of the palace unnoticed.

She wore her golden earmuffs and a thick woollen cape with its hood pulled tightly around her head, but she needn't have worried, the people of the kingdom had been scared into silence. Quiet police riding satin-shod horses patrolled the blanketed streets as the children played silently in the rain.

It was the children she was drawn to watching. She followed them as they ventured from the city streets out into the open fields. They looked at her questioningly but they did not object.

She followed them to the woods where they tumbled and rolled in the carpet of leaves and she lifted her golden earmuffs just a little, so the sound could rustle through her.

She followed them to the stream, where they paddled in the icy water, kicking and splashing and she lifted her golden earmuffs just a little, so the sound could bubble through her.

And finally she followed them to a cave. They were carrying lamps and baskets of sticks and they turned and smiled at her before they entered, inviting her to join their secret.

The cave swallowed up the children ahead of her. As the princess's eyes adjusted to the gloom she saw they were untying each other's gags. She felt their voices, heard their laughter spinning through her, despite her earmuffs. And slowly the children started to tap their sticks together and drum on rocks. The rhythm was beating, throbbing, pulsing, the children hummed in sweet, gentle voices, and the music rose through the stones of the cave until the princess could bear it no longer. She hurled her golden earmuffs into the shadows of the cave and lifted her voice to meet theirs for one ecstatic moment.

Then she shattered into a thousand shards.

Scattered on the floor of the cave, each shard sang a single note in the princess's clear, beautiful voice. And the children gathered up the shards in an old wicker basket, where they shone and sang, and the children sang too. And they carried the princess's voice out of the cave into the sunshine.

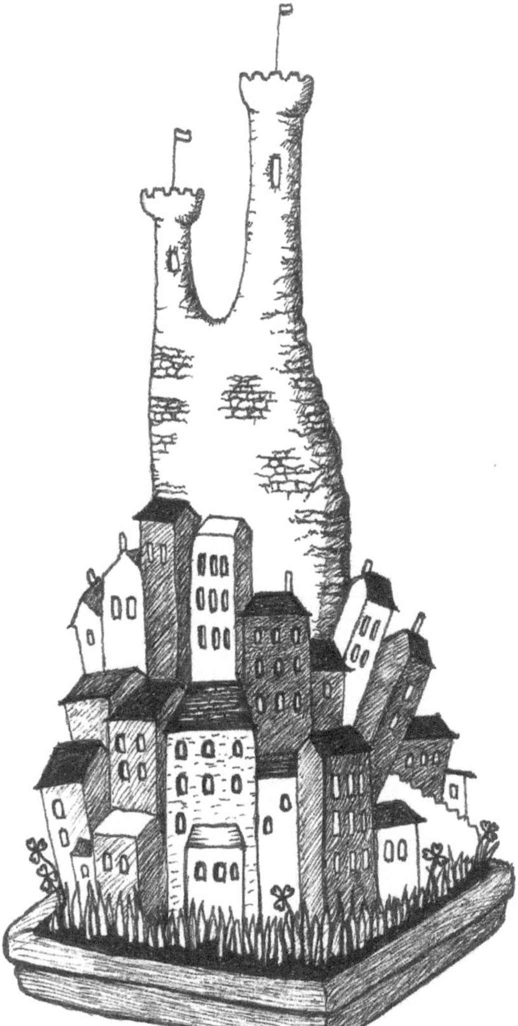

Growing Cities

The house was quiet. The radio in the corner that was always on wasn't on. The grown-ups were in the kitchen. They were being quiet. She pulled on the patio door handle and let herself outside.

Grandma's roses were full of bees. She ran down the path to Grandad's greenhouse. The glass was shining and there were raindrops on the inside. When she'd stepped into the soggy air she closed the door behind her, quickly but carefully.

There was a tray out on Grandad's workbench. His favourite stripy blue mug was next to it. She pulled out her crate for standing on. There was a gold-coloured moth floating in Grandad's tea. Should she pick it out or leave it there? Shouldn't touch hot drinks. She left the moth to swirl in the milky brown sea.

The workbench had all the things that Grandad needed on it: a green watering can, nail scissors, tweezers, spare trays. He kept a bag of compost with a spoon and a trowel in it underneath the bench. He kept the catalogue in the drawer, with some pencils and paper for writing things down.

The catalogue was one of her favourite things. It had pale yellow pages and it smelled like wrapping paper. She didn't know the words but there were special numbers next to a picture of each seed so that Grandad could write them down on an order form and put it in the post box to ask for more.

Had Grandad planted a seed in this tray? She poked at the soil with her little finger. It was quite wet. So there must be a seed in there. She watched. Nothing was happening yet. Sometimes it took a long time for a city to grow. First there would be a furry layer of grass. She wasn't allowed to touch it because you never knew when the bumps would spring out. The bumps were actually huts. And the huts were like wooden buds. And out of the buds came houses. She liked it when the houses got bigger but stone took a long time to grow.

Sometimes, when they came back another day, a castle would have appeared. And then there would be walls and towers and bigger houses, and lots of smaller houses and chimneys would sprout up round the outside. She stood right back when the tarmac roads came sneaking out of the soil like snakes.

Grandad let her collect the cobblestones that the cities shed in an old ice cream tub. They looked like dirty baby fingernails. Sometimes the tall chimneys fell down, sometimes their petals peeled off and there were glass towers inside. Grandad said there were lots of cities inside each city. She wished she lived in a city. Grandad said he did too.

The cities all had funny names that she couldn't remember. They sometimes grew differently but they always ended up the same. When a city started to die, Grandad put it in the shed.

She went to check the shed. No Grandad. She was allowed to leave the door open to the shed, so she could see. The little window was high up and dirty with cobwebs. There were lots of shelves in the shed. On the shelves there were old trays. Grandma said they had 'the carcrashes of cities in them.' When she asked Grandad what that meant he said 'like the chicken bones after Sunday dinner.'

She poked at a factory rooftop near the edge of a tray and her finger went through. She pulled it out carefully and sucked it. It smelled like burnt things and soil in the shed. There were spiders hiding in the cities. When they came in here she always said 'Why do the cities die?' and Grandad always said, 'Don't worry, we can always order another seed. Just don't tell Grandma.'

Grandad wasn't sad about the dead cities. He said everything leaves its mark. She ran back out into the garden to find him.

Glass, Bricks, Dust

AT THE TOP OF THE MOUND HE WAS KING. The brokenbrick, gravel and glass mountain had stood for over a year in a deserted street not far from the boy's house. When the excavators and bulldozers had come to demolish the old mill, a high metal fence had barricaded the site. But when the men in high-vis vests and hard hats disappeared with their machines, they took the fences with them. They left polystyrene cups balanced on top of the gateposts, where they filled with rainwater. They left the building's ribs—inner walls and doorways without doors. They left lumps of concrete, lengths of pipe, metal girders and fire exit signs. And they left the mound. As the days passed, rubble and red-brick dust spread onto the pavement and gathered in the gutters of the road.

On summer evenings he crept around the edge of the mound, toeing shards of glass and empty cider cans. He circled his kingdom, noting newly burnt lumps of wood and scrunched-up cigarette packets, but he never caught sight of the grown-up intruders who'd left them. There were lazy red butterflies on the tangle of flowering weeds that had pushed through the building's remains. Black birds gathered on the street's only lamppost before darting off overhead. He clambered up the mound, which looked like an enormous sand dune against the bright blue sky. From up there he could see the whole town: rows of terraced roofs, two church steeples, the town hall clock, and the last mill chimney with its luminous supermarket sign. At his back were the moors and the wind.

One evening, the boy was crouched on the top of the mound making a new town out of a heap of broken glass. He liked this time of day best—after tea, before bed. The air seemed to get grainy as its colour changed from vinegary yellow to candyfloss blue. He could rub it between his fingers like dust and slow time down. At the top of the mound he was in charge and he didn't want to go home to bed. He collected green glass shards and broken brown bottle necks. He tumbled fragments of old window in his hands like shattered marbles. He pushed the glass into the mound, making houses, balancing roofs on them, building towers. The last of the sunlight caught and glinted in the tiny glass walls.

More of the black birds than he'd ever seen before rushed overhead and gathered on the lamppost. The orange light hadn't yet switched on but the shadows were growing. He heard nine chimes of the town hall clock. For a moment, the lamppost looked like a tall thin man wearing a large black hat. When the man turned towards him, he looked like a lamppost. The man had a greyish-green coat speckled with rust and a black hat that quivered with beaks and feathers. The man didn't need to climb the mound; he was face to face with the boy with his feet still planted in the pavement.

'What are you making?' asked the man.

The boy didn't answer.

'It would be better to tell me. I could help. Every child is always making something. Cut them open and shake them out and they're full of dust and dreams.'

The boy squirmed at the mention of cutting. He stood up, ready to run, but then he remembered that at the top of the mound he was king. He dug his heels into the rubble. 'I'm making a new town, better than this one. The sun can shine in through the walls. The buildings look grander. It'll be a great glass city.'

'All it needs is people,' said the man.

'Yes, it needs people,' said the boy. And when he looked down, tiny creatures were scuttling beneath the glass roofs. They looked like ants or spiders, but the sky was darkening and the creatures were moving too fast to be sure. He looked to the man but there was only the lamppost and as its orange light snapped on, the birds launched into the sky.

The boy plunged down the mound and ran, hoping he wouldn't get told off for being late home. Before he reached the end of the street he knew something was wrong. The world was too quiet. Where were the sounds of cars? Of footballs being kicked against walls? Of smokers chatting outside the pub? There were no shouts from parents calling everyone in.

'Mum?' He pushed open their front door. The house was in darkness but the telly was switched on. His mum wasn't in any of the rooms. A half-drunk cup of tea had been left on the arm of the settee.

The boy thundered back along the silent streets. He stood in the orange light beneath the lamppost. 'Give them back,' he shouted.

Nothing happened, although he could hear the rustle of feathers coming from the darkness above the light.

The boy ran to the top of the mound. 'Give them back!'

'But I haven't got them.' The man's face glowed. 'You have.'

In the gloom, it was hard to make out the tiny creatures beneath the glass roofs. They were no longer moving. The boy couldn't be sure what was a particle of rubble and what was a person sleeping in their broken-glass house. 'How do I get them back?' he asked.

But the man was a lamppost again.

The boy crouched at the top of the mound and looked out at the night-dark shapes of the town. If he made the town as it really was, an exact replica, maybe that would bring everyone back.

He worked all night, building with bits of old brick. The clouds overhead moved slowly and their bellies were orange. Every time he looked up and caught a glimpse of a star, a bird flew from the lamppost to blot it out.

When the dawn came, it was damp and grey and the boy's fingers were stained red with brick dust. He looked proudly at his miniature town, with its rows of roofs, two steeples and the last mill chimney. He peered into the glass town beside it and saw it was empty.

The boy skidded down the mound and ran home. The streets were still silent, but they would be so early in the morning. In the living room the telly was still on, the cup still on the settee arm. The boy pounded up the stairs, not caring if he woke his mum and got into trouble. But she wasn't there. Her bed was empty.

The boy raced back to the mound. There were an impossible number of birds gathered on top of the lamppost watching him. The light had switched off, ready for a new day. At the top of the mound, he peered into the little broken-brick houses. The gaps he'd left for windows were too small to let in much light; he couldn't separate any tiny people from the darkness.

He pressed his fingers into the grit and dust. He had to try again. He gathered small mounds of dust and emptied rainwater from the old polystyrene cups onto them. He moulded houses and steeples and the chimney and the tower for the town hall clock. The buildings were misshapen and muddy.

'Aren't you going to ask me to give you the people back?'

The boy looked up at the lamppost. The creak of its voice had disturbed its hat, and wings were thrust out here and there.

'No,' said the boy. 'I'm going to go and get them.' As his words touched the air it thickened with dust and as he rubbed it between his fingers he knew he could make himself small.

The boy was no longer at the top the mound, but standing in the dusty street outside his house. He looked up at the sky, trying to see the edges of the bigger town where there was a mound of rubble on top of which he'd built this town. But the sky was too wide. He walked through the doorway without a door to his house and found his mum, dust collected in the lines round her eyes, sitting in front of the greyish lump of the telly. 'Mum.'

She didn't look up. 'Don't interrupt, love,' she said, 'this is a good bit.' So he took a deep breath, and blew. He blew at the telly and at the walls and at the clouds of dust that surrounded him. He ran out into the street, climbed to the top of a mound of dust and he blew and he blew and he blew the town away.

At the top of the mound he was king. The ruins of the three small towns lay scattered at his feet. He could hear cars and footsteps and voices and the nine chimes of the town hall clock.

When the boy turned away from the mound and the lamppost, he found the streets were coated in dust.

Soft greyish-brown snow. He felt the gritty air between his fingers and knew that if he rubbed it he could slow time down. But he didn't want to be in charge again, at least not for a while.

He wanted to go home to bed.

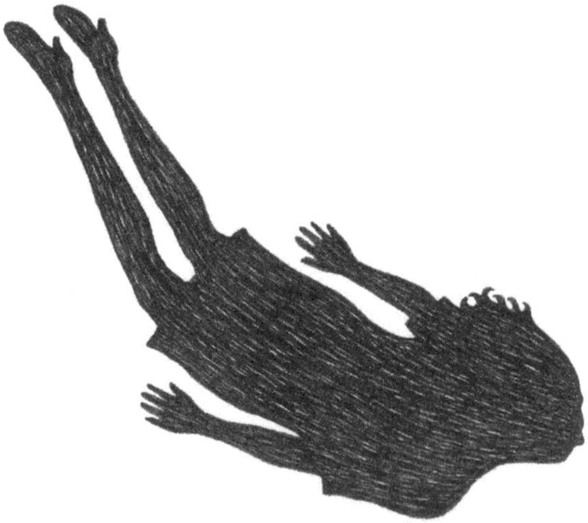

The Museum of Shadows
and Reflections

She hoovered sand, sweet wrappers and god knows what else from the red carpet every morning. The short, twisted fibres were a congealed, sticky mess. There were worrying dark patches here and there, and lighter ones where she'd had to use bleach to get rid of the smell of vomit. Hen parties in bunny ears and leg warmers were prone to vomiting. The management refused to replace the carpet with a red-painted floor. They said the carpet was 'integral to the celebrity experience' along with the faded velvet curtains and the hundreds of spotlights she had to check and dust each day.

When she'd done the entranceway, she moved through the rooms one by one, following the same trail that visitors took. She'd worked there fourteen years and she still got a thrill when she stepped behind the red rope barriers. She took a fresh pair of latex gloves from the pocket in her pinny. She had to be careful not to disturb the shadows too much. She'd taken to lightly blowing the dust from their shoulders and she used her wheely-step to reach the tops of their heads. They rippled in even the slightest movement of air. There was a painted screen set up behind each shadow and a floor spot sharply angled in front, so that to the visitors they were sharp silhouettes. There was more substance to them up close. Dense, threaded darkness with less definite edges. She let her fingers skim the surface but tried not to dip beneath it. No matter how carefully she cleaned them, the shadows were shot through with dust. They got thicker and heavier the longer they were there.

The reflections were different. They were much rarer and were treated like the crown jewels. Each reflection had its own room, and the encircling rope provided an even wider barrier from the public. A security guard, called Bill, paraded through their rooms during the day. She didn't have to clean the reflections because the dust slid right off them. She'd always found them to be disappointing things though, quivering and limp, their frozen features hazy.

She used a ewbank to do the carpets in all the rooms. Management were nervous about a hoover coming too close to any of their stars.

Mid-way through her shift she liked to stop for a brew. She always brought milk in—no one else did. The staffroom was a large cupboard with a sink unit and a small table in it. There was nowhere to sit. The walls were plastered in old posters from when the place had been called 'The Museum of Shadows and Reflections'. Management had decided the word museum sounded too old-fashioned and changed it to 'StarzWorld' a couple of years before.

Jada, one of the front-of-house girls, stuck her head round the door then swiftly disappeared and let it slam shut, almost catching a long, bleached lock of hair in it.

She'd been about to say 'Morning' to the girl, but she sipped her scalding tea instead. The young ones never had time for her, thought themselves above her no doubt. That would change if she got the front-of-house job that was going. When there'd been openings before she'd always filled out the application form then been told she was unsuccessful. Last time, though, they said maybe next time something came up the job would be hers. She was looking forward to greeting visitors as they came in. And to doing stints on the till in the gift shop selling reflection keyrings, shadow paperweights, and StarzWorld pink rock.

She filled the sink and washed her own cup and then all the others that had been used and left there from the day before.

The only room she'd been told she didn't have to clean was the archive. She always stopped in there for a bit though. In fact she paid it as much attention as anywhere else. She'd miss this room. There was no red carpet, no velvet drapes, no spotlights. Just rails and boxes crammed together in a small, dark-walled room. It smelled like her grandmother's wardrobe had when she was a child. There were no windows anywhere in the building, but in the archive the gloom was so thick you could rub it between your fingers.

Shadows sagging with dust hung on the rails. There were even a few precious reflections that had been deemed no longer fit for display. They should have shone with timeless youth, but they were distorted and shrivelled with age like crumpled yellow cellophane. How could someone give up their shadow or reflection? She still couldn't understand it. Management always said no one had ever been paid. So if they didn't do it for money it must be to do with wanting to be remembered forever. Would they still hand them over if they knew about this room?

She rifled through a box of old display labels. She often picked out names to research on the internet at the library. She wanted to be able to match the right label to each shadow and reflection, so that at least they'd have that. But some of them she couldn't find a trace of, like Edie Clegg. The label said hers was a real-life Cinderella story. That she was a beautiful young millworker plucked from obscurity by a big London director to star in his silent movies. He married her too, of course.

She spent ages searching for information about Edie and the films she'd been in. Then she found out that eighty percent of British silent films were lost. They'd been melted down to make waterproof paint.

For some reason, even though she'd never been able to find a picture of her, she was sure that Edie's was the shadow in the very back corner, on the far end of the rail that was furthest from the door. The shadow had short curled hair and narrow shoulders. When she held it up in front of her they were the same height. The rest of Edie was probably long since dead.

At the end of her shift, she hung her pinny up in the cleaning cupboard and propped the ewbank against the wall. There were no customers in the entranceway. It was still early. She got her bags and zipped her anorak up ready for the wind outside.

'Byeee,' Jada said. She was perched on a high stool behind the till, smiling, lips sticky with thick pink gloss.

It wasn't like Jada to be polite like that. 'Bye, love,' she replied.

'I just thought you should know,' Jada said, 'my friend Donna's starting here next week as the new front-of-house girl.'

'Oh, right, thanks. I've just…'

She turned and walked back into the building and mumbled, 'Forgotten something.'

The wind hit her as soon as she stepped out through the doors onto the prom. The sea was choppy and brown beneath the flat grey sky. A few gulls circled over the strings of dead light bulbs that crisscrossed the road. The road itself was closed and fenced off for building work, presenting a barrier to the sea that stretched as far as the North Pier. They were regenerating the front.

Most of the shops and takeaways on this stretch had their shutters down or were boarded-up. Tussauds, a bit further up, had a speaker system that advertised the names of all their stars on a loop. The faux cheery voice was louder than the builders' pneumatic drills. She slowed, trying to listen to a family who were arguing on the pavement.

'I want to go to the Sea Life Centre,' the youngest girl said.

'Mum, will you tell her, they've got Lady Gaga and Jeremy Kyle in here. And you can touch them.'

Touching was the big thing at Tussauds. She'd always thought it was better to have some distance from the stars, but now people wanted to grope them. They wore bits of the wax models away. She'd heard that Tussauds melted down old models to repair the popular ones. The family went inside, the little girl placated with the promise of a photograph with Cheryl Cole.

It was starting to spit, but she took her time: she had a lot to carry and there was no rush to get home. John wouldn't miss her as long as she was back in time to heat up a pie up for his dinner. She stopped to look at the tiny glass slippers and hearts in the window of the crystalware shop. She loved the way they sparkled, catching the light from god knows where on grey days like this. A digger started up, and she walked on. The smell of fried onions mingled with the drizzle. It was coming from a burger and hot dog stall in the entrance to one of the amusement arcades. She could hear the dinging of all the fruit machines as she walked past. The place looked empty.

The few touristy shops that were open had put umbrellas out for sale alongside the buckets and spades. Bags of pink and blue candyfloss were battered by the wind. The noise of the drills was constant. As well as not being able to get near the sea, she couldn't even hear it. Men in high-vis vests paraded up and down, and more diggers drove through. Piles of rubble had been abandoned everywhere. It looked like they'd been washed up by a high tide.

There was scaffolding all round the tower. They were just adding another layer of paint, she thought, another layer that would crack and peel away in the salt air.

The only way she could get near the sea was to walk out along the North Pier. She liked the North Pier much better than the Central one. It had ornate Victorian benches that ran almost the whole length of it. She walked through the left hand entrance so she could avoid all the clanging and flashing in the arcade. She stopped beneath a hanging basket full of plastic flowers and peered down over the side. The sea looked like old dishwater with a soapy scum on it as it swirled and splashed against the sea wall.

Even on a grim day like this she wasn't alone on the pier. A young woman pushing a buggy strode past her. An elderly gentleman clinging to the rail stared out towards Central Pier. The empty big wheel looked like it spun faster from this distance.

She felt lighter with the boards beneath her feet. There was a spring to them where they were rotting. She could see slivers of sea in the cracks. The noise of the diggers and drills was fainter at last, but a speaker system that was strung along the pier blared out a country and western song. Ahead of her she could see pale, cleaner patches where boards had been replaced, up against pitted, lichen-encrusted planks. Around the rusty tram rails the boards were as green as grass.

At intervals along the pier there were small kiosks. They had beautiful, miraculously intact, blue glass round the bases of their domed roofs. When she was a child, and brought out along the pier as a treat, she'd always thought they looked like something from the Arabian Nights. She'd never been bought anything from them but they'd always been open then. Now, one was an abandoned ice cream parlour, another a shut-up sweet shop that still had trays of fudge behind the smeared glass of the window. Neat little labels advertised flavours like Malibu and Baileys. Further down one was all closed up but its sign advertised:

REGULATION DARTS 4 EVERY CHILD!
LADY PRIZE EVERYTIME!!

The song on the speaker system had changed to an up-tempo cover of 'What a Wonderful World'. She could just hear snatches of the sea beneath it. A pigeon flew overhead. The rain was coming down harder but she wouldn't turn back, she'd carry on to the end.

The song was gradually replaced with the hurdy-gurdy waltz of an organ. She loved the Venetian carousel. It defied its grotty enclosure with the garish sign advertising the Carousel Family Bar. It was a hidden treasure. There were miniature paintings of Venice all around the top of it, with gondolas and bridges. It didn't matter that half of the little golden light bulbs were burnt out, the carousel still shone.

It wasn't turning. There were no customers today. She couldn't even see an attendant in the booth at the side. There was a beautiful carriage on it drawn by white horses. She'd always wanted to sit in it.

She walked on, past the empty picnic tables, the stage door of the theatre and the deflated bouncy castle, to the fence that cordoned off the very end of the pier. It was only the fishermen who got to go past it. A lone rod stood there unattended. She knew she'd have to be quick, before whoever it belonged to came back.

At last she could hear the sea, the suck and slosh of it against the rusty old legs of the pier. She hadn't intended to bring so many of them away with her. Just Edie, really. She'd thought she might hang her up in the wardrobe at home, but that would have meant trapping her somewhere else. This would be better.

She pulled the crumpled reflections from her anorak pockets first. They caught like carrier bags on the wind and soon grew small against the horizon. Then she took the shadows one by one from her handbag and shopping bag. When she let go of the first it was too heavy with dust and it plunged into the waves below. After that she gave them a good shake out first, like damp washing, and then let the wind snatch them from her fingers. Edie, she took out last. The shadow felt almost warm in her frozen hands. She held it up, gripped it tightly. It would be too easy to keep hold of it, to carry it alongside her own. She heard the creak of footsteps on boards behind her. With a flick that almost carried her over the rail, she cast her off.

*All mirrors
are magic mirrors.*

Reflections

The Sand Ship

WE LIKED IT WHEN THEY BUILT THE SHIP. There was just a big sandpit at that end of the playground before. Sometimes there was dog dirt in it. But one Saturday morning, after we'd been to the shop with Dad so we could get our sweets and he could get his paper and his can, we got to the sandpit and there was a ship in it. Gypsy said it must have sailed there in the night. I told her they'd built it during the week while we were at school.

We claimed the ship. It was painted red, and it had portholes in its sides. It had a gangplank you could walk along, up to the ship without touching the sand. I said I would be the captain and Gypsy could be the crew if she obeyed my orders. First I made her scrub the deck to get rid of all the sand, so we could lay our penny sweets out. I always got cola bottles, fried eggs and gummy bears. I pointed at a big fat seagull that was watching us from the fence, and nicked one of Gypsy's flying saucers when she looked up at it. Dad was sat on the blue bench over by the football pitch, reading his paper, so she couldn't tell on me anyway.

A little boy tried to come up on to the ship. His mum was at the other end of the playground, pushing a baby on the swings, so I blocked his way. I told Gypsy to pretend she had a hook hand. He jumped down into the sand and ran right to the edge of the sandpit. He crouched there and stuck his hands in, started to dig. He kept looking up at our ship when he didn't think we were looking at him. I saw him pull something green from the sand. 'Ben, time to go,' his Mum shouted. He buried it again. Gypsy had to dig for a long time to find it when he'd gone.

It was our first treasure. It wasn't like the glass we normally found at the playground. It was all scratched so you couldn't see through it, and it wasn't sharp but smooth like a stone. When Dad shouted us to go, we buried it and pressed two sticks into the sand on top of it.

The next Saturday there were lots of seagulls perched on the side of the ship. They flew up into the air when the playground gate clanged shut and we ran round flapping our arms and squawking to keep them away. I told Gypsy to dig for our treasure and I ran up the gangplank. The ship had been attacked. There were drawings and writing all over the insides, done in black felt tip pen. When she saw them, Gypsy said they must be pirate names.

There were cans, too, the same as Dad's. I tipped one up and the last of the smelly brown liquid dribbled onto my fingers. They were sticky for ages, even after I'd wiped them on my jeans. I told Gypsy to come and throw the cans overboard. Then, because she still hadn't found our treasure, I went to show her where to dig.

We couldn't find the glass. We shouldn't have left an X marks the spot on it. Someone else must have dug it up. Sand hurts when it gets too far up behind your nails, so I watched Gypsy dig deeper and deeper. She pulled a long dark rope of seaweed from the sand. It smelled funny, a bit like the fish section in Morrisons. Gypsy wanted to take it home, but I wouldn't let her because it would have made our room stink.

Other Saturdays, we found other treasures. Lots more glass, my favourite pieces were pale pink, and the best thing was the shells. When we took them to Dad, he said they were cockle shells. Said the council must have saved themselves some money by lifting the sand from a beach somewhere.

I laid the shells out on the deck to make pictures. When it was time to go, Gypsy buried them underneath the gangplank. But every time she went to dig them back up they weren't there, they'd been scattered all through the sandpit again.

It was a hot day when Gypsy first started worrying about the sand. Dad had bought us Mr Freezes. Mine was a blue raspberry flavoured one and Gypsy's was pink. I was making a picture of an octopus on the deck with the shells. Gypsy wouldn't dig for more, she said the sand felt funny, it kept moving between her fingers. She was sat next to me on deck when the boys came into the playground with their bikes. They circled round a few times then dumped them by the gate. They ran up and down the slide and pushed the swings so hard they flew up over the bar. When they ran up the gangplank Gypsy put her hands over my picture.

'What's that supposed to be?'

I didn't say anything. Through the nearest porthole I could see Dad wasn't looking, he was reading his paper. I wondered if I should shout.

'Looks like a cat with a lot of dicks to me,' the shortest boy said.

The other two laughed. Then the boy who hadn't said anything walked right up to the picture and stamped on it. Gypsy got her fingers out of the way just in time. He stamped and stamped and stamped until the shells were in tiny pieces that slipped into the cracks between the planks of the deck.

When they'd rode off on their bikes Gypsy tried to dig the slivers of shell out and one piece stuck in her finger like a splinter. She had to pull it out with her teeth.

After that, whenever we got to the playground, Gypsy wanted to play on the slide, or the climbing frame, or, when they weren't tangled up, the swings. She didn't want to play on the ship any more and she couldn't stand on the sand without falling over. I still liked the ship. I wasn't going to let some stupid boys take it. I guarded it from them and the little kids and the seagulls by myself.

It was a drizzly, windy day when Gypsy saw the tentacle. She was standing at the top of the slide and she screamed and screamed. I couldn't see anything. Dad came running.

On the way home, Dad wouldn't hold her hand even though she was crying. He said she was stupid, that she'd scared him half to death. It had just been a bit of black bin bag or something blowing in the wind.

When the wind blew the ship creaked. I liked watching it make waves in the sand. I wasn't going to give it up, but it wasn't as much fun without Gypsy. I told her she could have two of my penny sweets if she came and sat on it with me, then I tried saying she could have half my bag. She still wouldn't come.

It was a Saturday morning when there were no leaves on the trees. The sand looked wet. I jumped down into it from the ship and pretended I was sinking. I shouted 'help' just loud enough so that Gypsy would hear but Dad wouldn't.

She came running, but as soon as she stepped on to the sand I jumped back up on to the gangplank. I was laughing. She plunged downwards, so that only the top half of her was sticking out. She screamed and fought the sand, flinging her arms about. There was sand in her eyes and it coated her teeth and tongue. I screamed too.

Dad's paper blew away in the wind. I saw it fly overhead with the seagulls. He left his can on the bench. He ran towards us so fast I thought he was going to take off. He jumped into the sandpit and sank straight down. His head went beneath the surface, but he battled against the waves of sand and managed to push Gypsy out onto the gangplank.

We stayed there screaming until the old lady and the man with the dog came and told us to get down. Everyone says Dad can't have drowned in the sand, but I know he did.

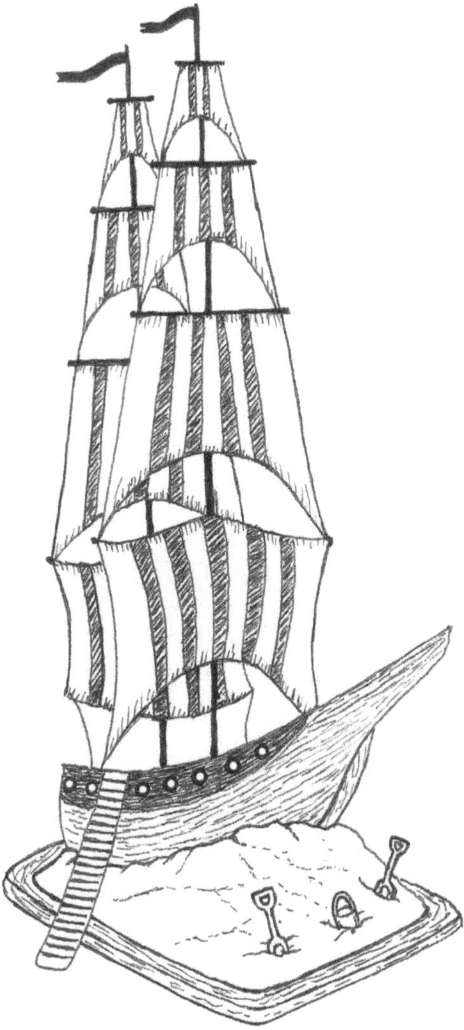

Moth Light

All winter, she'd stood on the platform after work and looked up at the lighted window. She was drawn to the glow. Not too bright, not too dim. There were books on low shelving units, their edges pressed against the glass. She could see canvases on the wall but she couldn't make out the pictures. The window was always lit but she never saw anyone inside the flat. She imagined what it would be like to live there, beside the noise of the trains. To look out and watch the commuters, veiled behind the wall of their clouded breath.

Now she was in the window. Charles was away, so she overrode the timer on the lamp switch and sat in the twilight watching commuters she'd probably once stood beside. Their camouflage of hats, gloves and thick coats now shed, she didn't recognise any of them. She kept the window open even when the room grew chilly. Behind the triple glazed glass, she was unnerved by the approach of silent trains.

The night she met Charles, she accepted the invitation back to his place without knowing where he lived. Her thoughts were warm and sticky from drinking too much Glühwein at the Christmas market in St Peter's Square. The sky was thick with orange snow clouds and the puddles in the road twinkled. The illumined shop windows they walked past looked like doors in a giant advent calendar. He tucked her under his arm. His beard tickled her ear as he whispered how beautiful she looked.

When they stepped into the relative darkness of the side streets and alleys, she lost all sense of where they were. They passed underneath the railway bridge, but she didn't click until they'd climbed the stairs of the building and he pushed open the door and led her into the room and she saw the light. She looked down to the platform below. Her mind lurched. It was like looking into a mirror and seeing behind the reflection.

Charles proposed to her by the window on New Year's Eve. 'I know it's insanely soon, but I can't be without you,' he'd said. And she'd believed him.

The Barrow train pulled in below. The train she used to catch home after work. She waited for the magic trick: when it pulled away again the crowd on Platform 2 had vanished.

A moth fluttered through the growing gloom. An insubstantial thing; like a scrap torn from a shadow. Her grandma had always said moths were made of dust and that they ate holes in clothes until the fabric fell apart. The plague and punishment of the lazy housewife. It dived at her and she flapped her arms. It had flown straight at her breast bone. She didn't see it fly away.

Charles didn't read the books that were pressed against the window. They were all doorstoppers, chosen for their girth. Their spines were uncracked, the pages unturned. Thrillers, historical romances, true crime. There was nothing there she wanted to read. The canvases she'd been able to see from the platform were covered with an insipid block pattern, just a shade lighter than wall. She'd brought boxes of her stuff with her, but if she put something out, like the red vase she put on top of one of the bookshelves, he'd say it looked out of place.

She started to see more moths in the flat, during the day as well as at night. She tried to catch one by cupping her hands around it, but when she opened them it had gone. Remembering her grandma's words, she stamped on another, but could find no remnant of it on her sock. Another flew right at the bridge of her nose, between her eyes. She smacked at it, but it disappeared.

She spent more and more time in the bathroom, away from the window and the moths. When she first moved in she found women's toiletries already in the cabinet. Charles had been incensed when she asked him about them, so they remained at the back behind hers. One evening, as she smoothed on some body cream, her nail caught on a skin tag just below her left breast. It hadn't been there before. She wiped the steamed-up mirror so she could examine it. She pulled at it and it slipped out too easily. It was a fleshy silver thread between her nails. As she held it up to the light it moved. She flushed it down the toilet and slammed the lid shut.

When the holes started to appear, Charles didn't mention them. He disappeared on business for weeks at a time. She rang in sick and spent hours watching the trains. She imagined walking down the stone station steps that glittered under the grimy fluorescent light. Standing on the platform she wouldn't look up at the window but out over the converted-warehouse rooftops, past white-lit office block signs. She'd listen for the rumble of the train's approach at her back, and then step up into the crush of warm bodies.

She rubbed at the impossible holes and traced their edges with her fingertips. When she pushed her fingers into them she felt nothing.

The holes had opened out into each other now, so she could stand with the light on without fear of being seen. A woman in a long white summer dress glanced up from the platform below. When she'd looked up at the window had someone else been standing there as she was now? A woman falling apart, the light shining right through her, not too bright and not too dim.

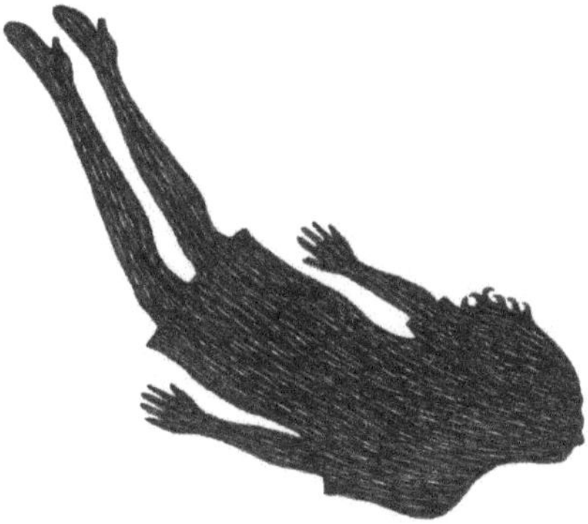

Stone Sea

RIVELYN WAS THIRD ON MY LIST IN A MORNING. It was just a thirty minute appointment and I had to be careful not to run over or I got caught in the traffic on the A6. She was one of the better ones. She opened the door to me without any fuss. She looked at me like she knew who I was. She'd always made an attempt to get herself dressed and she smelled clean, of Imperial Leather soap. It's too easy to miss the little signs that all's not quite right when you're dashing in and out, and getting the kettle on, and counting out the right number of tablets, and checking the sink and the bin for evidence they've eaten something.

Rivelyn wasn't a talker and I didn't push it. She had eyes that looked like the blue had been rinsed out of them. The first time I visited her she took me straight down the hall into the back room. There was a wing back chair in there and a small settee and an ancient-looking telly. The cushions on the settee were pristine, like they'd never been sat on. The telly was switched off. There were no photographs on the walls and from that I decided she'd never had children and probably hadn't been married. The view from the window was of her wheelie bins and the yard wall. The house looked clean enough but the air was stale and heavy. In most of their houses the silence is broken up by the ticking of a clock but in Rivelyn's house it lay thick and undisturbed on everything.

After I'd been going there a few months, she opened the door one morning and mumbled that she still needed to do her teeth. There was a tiny spot of toothpaste in the corner of her mouth but I didn't say anything. I watched her on the stairs. She was slow but she still seemed steady enough.

I was standing right beside the front room door, which was always shut, so I thought I'd take a peek. In older generations, of course, one room was often kept for best. And it's not unusual for my lot to confine their movements to one room for most of the day; the night, too, when they can no longer manage the stairs. The door knocked against something and wouldn't open fully. I poked my head around it.

If there had ever been furniture in the room it wasn't there any more. Underneath the window, running the length of the wall, was a promenade of stone buildings. These weren't like dolls houses and they weren't like those Lilliput Lane houses some of my others have lined up along their mantelpieces. The buildings looked too intricate, too real to have been carved or moulded. I crept around the door. I was careful to keep my feet on the navy carpet and not to touch the stone beach which spread out in swathes across the room. There were big hotels and a row of shops with frilled stone canopies.

I realised there was another street hidden behind the prom. The houses and shops there grew into the wall. The white anaglypta wallpaper had split and buckled around their roofs.

There was a stone sea wall and steps down on to the beach, where tiny pebbles had been tumbled till they looked more like glass beads than gravel. A pier stretched out along the carpet on thin stone legs. There was a carousel near the end of it, a silent organ at its heart. Stone horses frozen midair.

I found Rivelyn in the back room. She didn't question where I'd been. 'Would you like me to put the telly on for you, love?' I asked. I wanted to break up the silence, the memory of all that stone with some normality. She didn't answer, just sat staring into the middle distance. I turned it on and Jeremy Kyle's blather rushed into the room.

I kept the stone seafront to myself, in part because I didn't know where to begin in describing it to someone and in part because I was drawn to it. I didn't want anyone coming in and taking it or her away. I started slipping in there at some point during every visit and there was always more to explore. There was a shop with a sign that said Aladdin's Cave; there were slivers of stone postcards in racks on display outside its door. Some mornings, tables draped with stone cloths had been put out in front of one of the tearooms. The harbour wall was often left peppered with stone lobster pots and I'd find the occasional lone fishing boat stranded on the carpet.

Over the next few months Rivelyn talked less than ever. Her eyes were constantly focused somewhere past me. Her movements were stiff and she looked more unsteady on the stairs. I started plating meals up for her, to keep her going till I came in the next morning.

She sat perfectly still in her chair while I dashed about. There was grainy grey dust now on the mantelpiece and on top of the telly. 'Did you used to go on holiday to the seaside?' I asked her once. She didn't respond. 'I've always loved the seaside,' I said. 'We used to go to Rhyl every summer when I was little.'

As time went on the stone beach spread further, as though the tide of carpet was slowly going out. Sometimes the stone glistened as if wet and the air smelled almost salty, but I never saw any water. I began to worry about the floorboards, about the weight of it all pulling the house down.

I only saw Rivelyn look into the room once. She was agitated, as though she was looking for something, but she didn't say what. I watched as she bumped the door open and peered in. She stumbled back. She looked horrified. She pulled the door closed with a strength I didn't think she had.

One morning, she didn't answer the door. It happens sooner or later with all of them but it still gives me a little jolt every time it does. I peered in through the letterbox and I could see that the door to the front room was open. I ran to get the spare key from the neighbour, an elderly woman herself who spent an age sorting through various keys in a welsh-dresser drawer, trying to decide which one it was.

I think I expected to find Rivelyn collapsed in the room. Her bone-thin body propped awkwardly between the seaside streets. But the room was empty. The air felt clean and light, no longer dragged down by the stone and the silence. But the carpet was damp. I checked the whole house but there was no sign of her.

I went outside to call the care company. It was a sunny day. A fat seagull watched me from the rooftop opposite. I swear I could hear a carousel on the breeze.

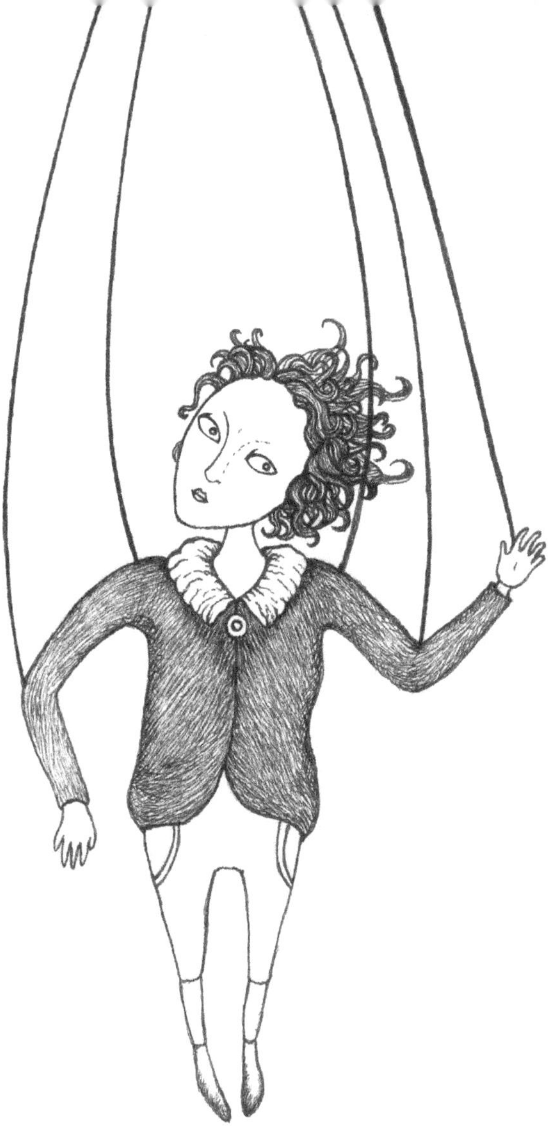

Marionettes

Karl wanted to keep looking for the American bar they'd had breakfast in seven years ago. It had been winter then. They'd stumbled into its warm fug from snow coated cobbles. It was spring now, and dusk.

'Can we just have a quick look in here first?' She lingered in front of the marionette shop's window.

He kept walking. 'I'm starving.'

'I don't know why we have to find that particular bar.'

'Because I liked their omelettes! I don't feel like eating dumplings and cabbage. It's too warm.'

The window of the shop was barely lit. From the dim glow, a gathering of witches, flanked by shadows, peered out at her. It looked like a page from a storybook. 'You wouldn't let me look in here last time.'

'We never even saw this shop.'

'We did.' She moved towards the entrance and ducked slightly, ready to step beneath the jester marionettes strung from the doorframe. 'Please.'

Her heels clicked on the stone floor. The shop stretched back much further than she'd expected it to, a white walled cavern of dangling heads, legs and arms. It would be impossible to say the shop was empty because there were so many eyes watching her. There was no sign of a shopkeeper, though. No other customers. She glanced behind her and saw Karl's bulk silhouetted in the doorway.

The marionettes hung in tiers. She stuffed her hands into her coat pockets to stop herself touching them. Chiselled contours gave them impossibly soft looking skin that rucked and wrinkled as though it stretched and sagged over bones. Each character's expression looked impermanent, as though it would shift the second you turned away.

'Look at this thing.' Karl stood behind an antiquated till.

'Don't touch it.'

There were more witches like the ones in the window, a row of wizened faces. She tried to avoid their canny gaze. There were simpering princes and princesses in medieval dress. Smiling devils thrust out bulbous tongues. But there were contemporary characters too. The attention to detail was amazing. One elderly man in a cagoule stooped under the weight of the rucksack on his back. A small boy in a perfectly miniaturised football shirt and shorts had grazed knees.

'Right, come on, you've had a look at the puppets now. We've been in Prague two hours and I've not had a beer. That's madness.'

The next morning she left Karl in bed with his hangover. 'We're on holiday, we can actually have a lie in,' he'd said.

But when she opened the curtains on to a brilliant blue sky she wanted to be down on the cobbled street below. She couldn't tell him the thought of wandering the city alone thrilled her. She said she wanted to shop.

It wasn't quite nine and the Charles Bridge was already swarming with people. Jostled along in the crowd, she could barely see the sparkling surface of the Vltava, or the artists plying their work. Blackened statues punctuated the sky above the heads of American pensioners and Japanese students. There was a bottleneck in front of the statue whose bronze plaque it was lucky to rub if you wanted to return to the city. At the other end of the bridge rose the Old Town Bridge Tower. She remembered the view from the top of it in a biting cold wind, Karl with his coat unzipped wrapping her into it.

She entered the web of streets of the Old Town. Streets too narrow for the number of tourists that surged through them. Occasionally, she paused before a doorway or a sign and had the impression she'd stood there before, but with Karl, and talked about buying tickets for that recital, wondered where that alleyway led. The jumble of memories was confused by the fact that so many of the shops and passages looked the same, repeating themselves along with the cobbles.

When she came to the marionette shop she stopped. She hadn't realised she was so close to it. She'd already passed several other marionette shops that had cheap-looking Pinocchios in garish costumes dangling outside. This was a proper marionette shop. The scene in the storybook window had changed. The gaggle of witches had gone and there were now just two marionettes behind the glass: a man and a woman. They had pale faces and dispirited eyes. They were both dressed in jeans. The man had a black coat on, the woman a green one. She touched her fingers to the glass as she realised it was a perfect, hand-stitched miniature of her own. The woman had brown eyes with dark shadows beneath them. Her eyes. And there was a line etched into her forehead between her brows. Karl reminded her about that line whenever he saw her frown. The man had Karl's blue eyes, his mousey, receding hairline. The scar in his eyebrow from a teenage piercing. His marionette had hold of the string just above her marionette's hand.

'It was us.'
'Don't be ridiculous.'
'It was. They looked just like us.'
'No one can carve a puppet that fast.' He'd still been in bed when she got back to the hotel and was only just pulling on his jeans. 'And anyway there was no one in that shop last night to see us.'
'Your marionette had hold of one of my marionette's strings.'
'Well, that's definitely not us then—you do all the string pulling.'

'Just let me show you.'

They were planning to go to the castle so they could have lunch in the café with the vines painted on the ceiling, but a quick walk into Old Town wouldn't take long. They joined the stream of tourists on Charles Bridge. As they reached the Old Town Bridge Tower she saw Karl glance up at it but he didn't say anything. Her pace slowed as they wound through the alleyways. What if she'd been wrong? Or made too much of it? He'd love that. She paused outside shops selling wooden toys saying they should get something for the children, although she knew they'd prefer something overpriced and plasticky from the airport.

'Are we nearly there yet?' He stuck out his bottom lip in perfect imitation of Meg, their youngest.

'It's just down this way. I remember that door.' The arched wooden door was studded with ironwork. She didn't admit they'd already passed several very like it.

'Have you got the guidebook with you?' He looked like he'd had enough.

'I didn't pack it. I didn't think we'd need it. That shop wasn't in the book anyway.'

They trawled the rambling maze of passages. When they emerged at one point into the Old Town square, the sudden space and light above made her think of a glade in a forest. There was no escaping the crowds though. They passed the black house with the strange white sgraffito figures on the walls. A knot of people stood before the Astronomical Clock. There was an appreciative exhalation from them as the little Death dinged his bell. The parade of wooden characters began. Karl strode on, past the little huts where they'd bought a Christmas bauble that had long since smashed, past the van selling mulled wine—it smelled cloying in the warm spring air.

A horse and carriage made lackadaisical progress round the square. An older couple sat in the back, a blanket on their knees, holding hands.

'It's not this way,' she said. 'We need to go back into the lanes, back towards the river.'

'How can you tell which way the river is?'

She walked ahead now and he trailed just behind. When she felt his presence missing she turned. He'd stopped in front of a window full of tarnished silver jewellery set with garnets, or maybe red glass.

'I bought you a ring from here.'

'You did. You didn't want me getting too many ideas, said it could be our engaged to be engaged ring.'

'Where is it?'

'I had to stop wearing it when Charlie was born. I was scared I was going to catch him with it.' She had no idea where she'd put it. Somewhere safe. 'Come on, I give up, let's forget about the marionettes.'

When they got to the castle complex and finally found the café with the vines on the ceiling, it was closed for refurbishment. Karl didn't say anything, just stalked back the way they'd come. As they passed through the courtyards she tried to take in the grandeur, the gothic palaces, the ornate mass of St Vitus's cathedral that towered over everything. 'Don't you want to look at any of it before we go?'

'We've seen it all.'

Outside the gates, he stopped by the low stone wall. The red-roofed, blue-domed, grey-spired city spread out below them. The woods of Petřín Hill rose across from them, dark against the skyline. The Observation Tower pierced the canopy.

'We've stood here before,' he said.

'Yes,' she said. 'We had an argument about a flag.' She couldn't remember why. 'Does the view look different to you?'

'We were different then.'

The next morning she packed their things. She tucked empty bottles into the bin beneath some tissues, trying to disguise the fact Karl had drunk everything in the minibar. A tradition. She made the bed. They left their bags at reception saying they'd collect them later.

Karl had suggested they visit Petřín Hill. It was a drizzly day. As they walked through Malá Strana, along an uncharacteristically wide road, she didn't want to admit to herself that some of the pale pink and grey stone buildings looked drab. There was graffiti on the wall of a chemist's. Trams whirred past.

Too impatient to wait for the funicular railway, Karl led the way up a steep woodland path. Every so often, he'd pause beside a tree on the pretence he was taking in the view. She remembered him carving their initials. It wasn't into a tree, it was a tree stump. She was sure she wouldn't have let him do it on a living tree.

Near the summit, they came to a stop on a grassy knoll. The air was damp and chilled. She wished she had a scarf. The castle was across from them. They were looking at the place they had stood the day before. She almost wanted to wave to the memory of them, or at the memory of them stood there years before, to distract them from a pointless argument about a flag.

On the descent they skirted the crenellated Hunger Wall. The whitish stone was stained with patches of lichen. Sodden mulch gave way beneath her feet.

'We should get a drink before we have to get back for the transfer,' Karl said. He must have given up on the trees.

She left him in a bar. Told him she still needed to pick up something for the children, something really from Prague, not just from the airport. Being pressed between the multitude of bodies and chatter on the streets of Old Town felt almost comforting after the stark quiet of the hill. She ambled round gift shops, fingered bright wooden animals, snow globes with miniature castles inside, tubes of colouring pencils. She eventually settled on a wooden duck and a crocodile. Each was wrapped in its own paper bag. She stuffed them into her handbag, which then wouldn't zip up, and stepped back out into the drizzle.

It seemed she could only find the shop when she wasn't looking for it. She headed down a narrow passage that she thought would take her back to the bar and found herself in front of the familiar, dimly lit window. There was now only one marionette behind the glass, hers. She felt a strange release. A nervous weight settled between her chest and her stomach. The eyes of the marionette had more depth to them than paint on wood should allow. Tiny blood vessels crowded the whites at the inner corners. The indent of the frown line on the brow had softened. The arm strings were slack, the hands tucked into the coat pockets. She saw her own reflection overlaying the marionette that in turn mirrored her. She had her hands in her pockets.

She stepped back. Where had Karl's marionette gone? Maybe he had got there before her, bought them both as a surprise. He was inside, and any minute now the shopkeeper's hand would reach her marionette from the window to wrap it and place it in the bag alongside his. She shrank back across the alley and shielded herself in the doorway opposite. It was a ridiculous fantasy but she waited. Rain dripped from the eaves and pattered on the cobbles.

The flow of tourists slowed to a trickle. The shadowy glow in the window faded and she realised that on her previous visits the shop door had never been shut. There had always been marionettes strung up above the doorway. There weren't today. She crossed and tried the handle. It was locked.

The lanes had emptied. Everyone else was sheltering from the rain in warm bars and tearooms. Faces watched her from the windows. She tried to retrace her steps but the tangle of passageways disorientated her. Her handbag was collecting rainwater. The paper bags inside it were disintegrating and the vividly painted wood of the toys poked through. She jammed them further down and managed to get the bag to zip up. She strode on and tried to sense which way the river lay. There was a door studded with ironwork that she definitely recognised, but she turned a corner and soon met its double. Bewildered, she stepped into another passage. It was as though the daily flood of visitors carved new alleys and inlets into the already labyrinthine folds of the Old Town. Her heart beat faster as her heels struck the cobbles.

She was stood in front of the window again.

Her marionette remained in isolation on the bare sill, a crowd of shadows behind. Trying to smother her panic, she stared into her own eyes and willed the streets behind her to rearrange themselves, to let her go. Her breath touched the window and for a moment it hung on the other side of the glass.

Each raindrop found a new path down the pane. The string attached to her left hand had been pulled taut so that her palm was raised in a permanent wave. Faces peered in at her, bulbous and lined. A parade of witches and devils. No one waved back. The face she waited for didn't appear. The memory of his features dispersed into the flat grey picture of the world behind the glass. Behind her, the air stirred with silent breath and the beating of wooden hearts. She longed to turn around.

When she was lifted, the tug shivered through her scalp and hands and feet. She was swept across the stone floor to a recess near the back of the shop and strung up beside the elderly man with the rucksack. He was mute company. She could no longer see the window. In time she forgot it was there.

Chorden-under-Water

Chorden: an insignificant village at the bottom of an insignificant valley. Lawkhill, the place we used to pay our council tax to, is twenty miles away. They didn't care when we lost our post office in 2004, or the public house in 2008. Not that it was much of a loss. They didn't have a cleaner. The carpets smelled of wet dogs and stale beer. We only used to go in when Ada insisted. I'd just have a packet of cheese and onion crisps—their glasses were always smeared—but Ada would have a lemonade.

When they announced they were building the dam, there was no public outcry. The water was needed for Lawkhill and the big cities further south. Places we never had occasion to go to. There wasn't a local newspaper to make a fuss for us. The Chorden Recorder had been shut down in 1987 and it was a waste of time for years before that, nothing but advertisements and football. A lot of the people we grew up with had left the village long ago, or passed away. There were empty houses already, and the posh lot with their second homes were more than happy to take the money and go elsewhere.

Men in suits came and told me I had to sign things and then I was sent a cheque for the house and I put it in our money tin in the freezer. There's never been a bank in Chorden. There hasn't been one in Hopple, the next village along, since 1993. Lawkhill's got a street full of banks but they stopped our bus service there in 2002.

I try to keep to a routine. My mother was a great one for routines, always up and dressed with her full face on at dawn. Every day of the week had a purpose and each hour of the day was given to a different task. Monday was wash day. No need for that anymore but, still, a routine's important.

When I wake in the morning, the first thing I do is look out the window. I used to check the weather to see what to wear. Down here there are clear days and murky days. I have to sleep in the living room now because the stairs are lethal. The windows are glassless. The walls bare stone. The yellow embossed wallpaper that Ada picked survived longer than I thought it would, but in the end it began to lift and split. Strips of it twirled in the water like snakes before they floated off out the window. If you don't weigh things down here, they're soon gone.

The plaster crumbled not long after, falling to the carpet in clumps, trailing puffs of cloud. I swept it up as best I could. Of course the carpet was already long buried beneath the mud, but I like to sweep. Sometimes I do it until I've silted up the water so much I can't see. The remains of the curtains are still clinging to the curtain rail. Drowned rags. So sodden barely a tug of the water can budge them. A little like me.

It's surprising what survives down here. I've collected all kinds of little knick-knacks. I'm not a thief. I'm just taking care of the things that people forgot to take with them. Plant pots, chipped mugs, pans, a Rubik's cube, three rolls of sellotape. I've found books. In number 14 there was a whole bookshelf full of them. No one had lived in there since 2005 when Mr Durham died. Some of the books have little plastic labels stuck to their spines; they must be library books from Lawkhill Library. The pages are too soggy to be separated though.

Sometimes I find little treasures; an earring, a brooch, buttons, coins—lots of coins, mostly coppers but enough to buy several packets of cheese and onion crisps if I still had the opportunity. In number 6 I found three small glass bird ornaments on the mantelpiece and only one of them has a broken wing.

I don't bother with the big things. A lot of people left their cookers and there are bikes with missing wheels and wheelbarrows and broken ironing boards. Things move about too. One morning there was a child's red tricycle right outside my front door. I remembered seeing it before, over the wall of number 2. It was rusty even before the water came. There's a rabbit hutch in number 13's yard—I just hope they remembered to take the rabbit with them. Washing lines are still strung up.

It gives me a turn every time a plastic bag gets caught on one of them and I think there's a blouse blowing in the wind.

I've recently borrowed one of next door's green plastic garden chairs because our settee has turned to a bed of mush and metal spikes, crawling with life. The last of the dining room chairs lost a leg last week. But this plastic chair's a devil; it won't stay still. I go to sit down and it isn't where I left it. And I never hear it move. I can't hear a thing but the babbling of the water.

Once I'm up in a morning, and dressed, the next thing I do is go out for a little walk. I still shut the door when I leave the house. Well, I push it to—the wood's too swollen for it to shut properly. None of the houses have roofs now but I think it's nice that there are still walls and doors. Gives me a sense of privacy.

I walk in the road rather than on the pavement. It's like when we were children, never a thing on the street but us playing our games. Elastics and marbles. I've lived on this street all my life. Ada lived in number 3. I lived on the other side, number 12. When we got to courting age the old folks in the village used to tease us, asking what two pretty young girls like us were doing without husbands. When both our parents had died we sold those houses and bought number 7 to be our own. Ada was 44 and I was 43. No one bothered asking us about husbands again.

It didn't surprise me that I was able to stay. I've

never wanted to live anywhere else. It took a while for the river to burst its banks but when it did the water came swishing up the road and ferreting under the door. No one came to check the village was empty. They'd said they were going to demolish the buildings before they finished the dam but in the end they didn't bother. Must have decided to save themselves some money and let the water do the work for them.

Down here, my chest feels clearer than it has done for years and it's easier for me to stay upright in the water than it was in the air.

I enjoy the walk to up to the church, past the green. The war memorial cross is still standing, although, of course, the duck pond has gone. When we were girls the men would play cricket on the green. Serious business it was and woe betide any duck that waddled into their way.

We never played in the churchyard. Billy Chadwick told us it was haunted, that if we went near the stones, ghosts would appear and scratch out our eyes. The place looks untidy now. I try my best to keep on top of the tangle of weeds but they crawl into the cracks and curl round the stones. On Ada's grave I keep a bunch of plastic carnations under a rock. I borrowed them from number 3. I wish I had daffodils for her, but we have to make do. Sometimes when the sun's shining on the surface over my head and I'm kneeling there I fancy I can hear the bell ringing. But it's a trick of the water. They took the bell with them after the last service in 2009.

    On my way home I collect small pebbles and stones. I've worn through too many pockets with them already but I need to weigh myself down. What worries me is I'll die without seeing it coming, rise to the surface, and they'll fish me out and take me away.

    I couldn't bear to leave the village.

Casting Ammonites

She arrived just as a gull lifted from the sea—sprung from the tip of a wave, it did, salt frosting its sodden feathers. She was unexpected. I didn't see her stumble down the path, or linger peering into the huts, the way people do, as though no one lives here. Happen it's them wearing the place away with all their gawping, with all the pictures they take.

It was lip-splitting cold. One of those mornings when the dark clings to the edges of the sky waiting to rush back in. The light was stretched out thin across everything. I'd taken the boat out to drop the pots first thing. Baited them with mackerel. Left a constellation of buoys in the black water, a snare of ropes underneath. I lit a fire, but I can never get warm once the sea's touched my bones. In winter, if I sit here long enough I'm sure I'll turn to stone. Be some fossil hunter's prize discovery. They'll put me in the Whitby museum.

She was walking right on the cusp of the sea. Hadn't stopped to look at the rocks, to pick them up and feel the weight of years in them, to unclasp her fingers hoping to find curls of time in her palms. People only come here to take the stones. After a while, she took a step back from the sea, and then another. She had an old satchel, and from it she pulled out a sketch book and pencil—she'd come to take something after all. When the wind stripped the hair from her face I realised she was older than I'd thought. But it was only later, close to, I could see the lines round her eyes that outlasted her smile and the wiry grey curls budding in her dark hair.

I let her find me. She crouched on the sea-slick stones. Dipped her fingers into pools to retrieve skeletal seaweed and held it up, dripping, against the sky. She picked up stones but she didn't hammer them or try to split them apart like so many do. She didn't draw anything. She was putting the sketch book back into her satchel when she looked up and saw me. She turned away, back to the line of sea and sky. But she knew she was being watched. Her movements became more considered. She tried to keep her back to me.

It was the labyrinth that caught her. She half-skipped with delight, self-consciousness shed. Most who walk the beach don't find it. The labyrinth's stones are hidden in the seaweed. The path they mark out has to be felt through your soles as much as seen. Once she'd recognised it she walked around it rather than into it. Clever girl.

When the coil of stones was between us she looked up and right at me. The wind had taken up so much of her hair it seemed she was suspended from the sky. She wound back round the edge of the circle towards me.

'Hello,' she said, when she was close enough for me to hear her over the water.

'Hello,' I said. I waved a hand for her to come and sit beside me on the bench. People always wonder at there being furniture down here. They can't believe it was carried down the steep cliff path. Well, most of it wasn't. I'm waiting for a piano to wash up with the tide, crusted with so much salt and rust you have to crack its strings to get a note from it.

She sat, dragged her hair from the wind's reach and accepted the glass I'd been cradling. My best glass. Etched with sea air. Whisky tastes better from that than anything. Even the cheap stuff.

'Thank you.' Her voice cracked with cold and maybe a little with sadness. I couldn't be sure.

'You didn't draw anything,' I said. 'You did right. It's better that way.'

She took a sip of the whisky and let an ammonite fall from her hand to her lap. 'They're unsettling,' she said, 'the stones, I mean.'

'Snakestones.' Good for her, not calling them beautiful, like that lot with their windproof parkas and digital cameras do. They're not beautiful, these tight old knots of dead stone. 'It's St Hilda's work,' I said. 'The woman transformed a plague of snakes. There used to be a good trade in carving heads on them. Some people will do anything to make a story true.'

I lifted the stone from her lap and ran my finger along the cold outer ridges of the whorl. 'No one knows what they looked like,' I told her. 'The soft part, the outline of the body, never survived in stone. An ammonite lived in the mouth of its shell, built itself room after room as it grew, sealing each one off behind it.'

'So it could never go back.'

'No, it could never go back.'

She drained the whisky. That made me smile, though I was glad I hadn't got out the good stuff.

'Could I draw you?' She looked away as she asked, as if already expecting my answer.

'No, no, none of that. I'd probably turn to dust. Be nothing but pencil lines on the breeze. You've got to be careful who you let catch you.'

'You don't remember me, do you?'

I wasn't expecting that. I searched her face, the turn at the corner of her mouth. The light blue eyes—irises so pale they were in danger of slipping into the whites. 'No, I don't know you,' I said.

I took the glass and refilled it from the bottle I keep propped between stones under the bench.

'Your hut's being eaten by rust,' she said.

'It's growing another skin.'

I let my head rest back against the familiar grooves of metal. We sat with nothing else to say and everything unsaid and passed the glass between us. Minutes swelled. The sea slowed till it barely touched the shore.

The moment stretched right out to its bare bones and I felt a rare warmth sink into me. The turn, as with the tide, was almost imperceptible, but she roused and took back the ammonite she'd collected. Cast it onto the beach. The water returned to take it.

'Did you lay out the labyrinth?'

'No, it was here before I came. It's for catching trolls, bad winds, spirits. Fishermen have made them for centuries. Not so much now, perhaps.'

'Have you walked it?'

'No. I tend it. Watch over it.'

'What happens if I walk into it?' she asked. 'Do you lose me again?'

I shrugged, waved my hand. 'I don't know you. Sorry.' I didn't know what else to say.

Then she was on her feet, running, stumbling across stones fresh-licked by spray. And something tugged inside me. I could see her when she was young. I could feel her hand in mine. She was nearly at the labyrinth. If I could have tied her down with ropes I would. 'Come back,' I shouted, but I was spitting into the wind.

She followed the bight of the labyrinth, wound her way into it, right to the centre. For a breath, her defiance held back the rush of the tide.

I did remember her.

But already there's silt and saltwater collecting around her feet. There was a woman, a girl. What was I telling you?

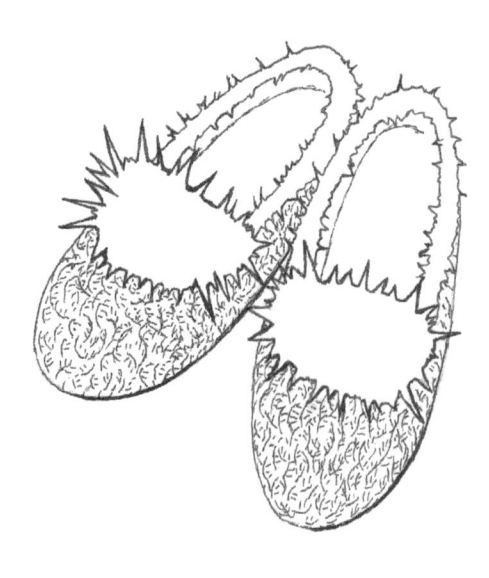

The Woman Who Wore Frost Slippers

THERE WERE THREE KNOCKS ON THE DOOR AND THEN silence. In the silence, the old woman struggled to rise from her chair. Her fleece-lined slippers scuffed against the hallway carpet. She let her fingertips trace a path along the wall—imagining a rail made it easier to stay steady on her feet. When she opened the door there was no one there.

This happened three nights in a row. The knock was hard and sharp, as if wood were rapping on wood. On the third night, the woman thought she saw the outline of a small girl against the copper streetlight, but the silhouette scuttled away and smudged into the darkness of the woods at the end of the road.

'How are you feeling today, love?'

The carer shouted through from the kitchen, where she was preparing meals for the next few days.

'No good. I'm aching all over.'

'Have you taken your tablets this morning?'

'No.'

The carer brought through a cup of tea. She continued to shout, as though she was still in the other room. 'Are you sure you haven't? The tub's just here beside you.'

'Have you seen a girl hanging about by my door? There's one been pestering me. Keeps knocking.'

'I haven't seen anyone, love.' She headed back to the kitchen, and raised her voice even more. 'Did you go out yesterday?'

'No. It was too cold.'

'Are you going to try to get out today? Have a little walk to the market?'

'No. I'm aching all over. Have you seen a girl by my door? There's one keeps pestering me.'

'I haven't, love.'

The old woman dozed off in her chair, leaving her tea untouched. She was roused by a hand on her shoulder. 'I'm leaving some new slippers for you, love. They might feel cold when you first pop them on, but I think they'll do you good. Help you move a little more easily. Brighten things up for you. They won't last long, though, try to remember that.'

'Nothing lasts now,' she muttered without opening her eyes. 'They don't make things properly any more.'

'I'll be in again on Thursday.' There was a clunk as the carer shut the front door.

The old woman didn't look at the slippers until it was time to get out of her chair and reheat the dinner that was waiting for her in the fridge. The carer had left the slippers on the windowsill, where they were somehow catching light from the grey day outside and spitting it back out in a shower of shine. She picked one up with great care. It looked as if the finest hoar frost and ice flowers had been scraped from wall-tops and window panes, and woven into its delicate crystal upper, while the sole seemed to be made from ice and light. The slippers were far, far too fancy for her gnarled old feet—and they'd be so cold—but she couldn't stop herself. She pushed her toes right into them, and the frost spread, growing up over the hard blue veins that made ridges beneath her tights. When she took a step she slid through the air just above the floor. Well, she didn't know what to think. She dropped the slowness of age like a heavy wool coat to the floor. Her shadow seemed to catch on the carpet a little, grumbling at having to keep up, but she whirled around the living room. She was free.

When the woman set off for the market she took a wrong turn. Whether it was the touch of north wind threaded into the frost slippers, or her own wayward memory, she couldn't be sure. She'd lived in the same house, and gone to the same market, all her life. But on that day, with her shopping bag clutched in her hand, and after only a handful of exhilarating steps, she found herself in the woods.

The bare branches above her shivered beneath the weight of cold air. She headed for the fairy path, delighting in each and every step she took. The fairy path climbed above the main path and curled around tree trunks. It was pocked with holes and stepped with crooked roots. When she reached a hollow tree, she stopped. She'd been here before, she was sure of it. The memory was hiding just beneath her thoughts, but she couldn't pull it up. 'Another dropped stitch,' she muttered, and set her shopping bag on the ground.

The tree was a hawthorn, with sharp thorns on its branches and not a hint of the blossom it would bear in the spring. In-between its tangled roots something long and white protruded from the ground, half-swaddled in dead leaves. She stooped to touch it. It wasn't a mushroom. It was cold and hard beneath her fingertips. She pulled at it and a small teapot emerged from the ground—child-sized, from an old china tea-set.

The miniature arch of a cup handle stuck up by her left foot. She pulled that out too. The cup was chipped and lined with leaf skeletons. The teapot was full of earth.

She lowered herself to the ground as carefully as she could out of habit. But she didn't need to because nothing ached any more. A fine powdering of frost had crept from the slippers up her tights. It collected in the wrinkles of beige nylon. Sunlight caught on the tips of her eyelashes, making prisms, and she almost remembered.

The tree hadn't always been hollow. She was sure it hadn't been hollow. A last lonely leaf from the branches above floated down and she caught it. A pale, tough little thing. She tucked it into her bag. Take a treasure to remember, her grandmother had always said.

She was about to pour the earth from the teapot when she heard footsteps scattering leaves. The girl was tiny, but she had to be wearing wooden boots for all the noise she made.

There was something about the child's face she didn't like. It was too familiar, but she couldn't remember it. And it wasn't quite right. Her smile was fixed, but her brown eyes looked sad. Her skin was the colour of faded leaves. The girl reached out a hand towards her. She's after my bag, the woman thought, and she leapt up. As she clambered away she found she was climbing through the air.

She scrambled up through the branches, rising higher and higher and higher until her feet skimmed the tops of the trees. The woods and then the town shrank below her. She skated over the rows of terraced houses that ribbed the hills. She could have reached down and pricked a finger on the church spires and mill chimneys. Higher and higher she went, until she was coddled by the clouds and she forgot the above and below and tomorrow and before.

The old woman walked with the wind high above the world until she felt hungry, hungrier than she'd ever been in her life. She stepped down onto a red-tiled rooftop in a great city of narrow streets and grey domes.

Ribbons of cloud were strung between the buildings. In the gaps she could see the sea.

There was a chair, a table, and some bookshelves on the roof, as though it were another room to be lived in. She sat at the table and her stomach groaned. A pigeon landed on the bookshelves, then another, and another. 'I have nothing to feed you with, I'm sorry,' she said. 'I'm famished myself.' All at once the birds took off into the air.

The pigeons returned with tiny pastries gripped in beak and claw. They dropped them onto the table before her—making a little mountain—but she took only three and left the rest for the birds. The pastries had almonds and walnuts and honey folded deep inside them. A great storm of grey wings erupted around her as more and more birds joined them. When it cleared there was a single white feather left amongst the pastry crumbs. She tucked it into her bag—take a treasure to remember—and closed her eyes to listen for the sea. There were wooden footsteps on the cobbled street below. She's come for me here, too, the old woman thought. Well, she'll not get me. And she clambered back up to the clouds.

The world flattened out below her. She skipped across countries like fingers across a map. She didn't want to forget this lightness. She left the endless sky only when she was thirstier than she had ever been before.

The old woman stepped down from the sky onto the cold, hard pebbles of a lakeside. The water shone darkly beneath the stars. This was the daytime darkness of a far northern country. She kneeled, cupped icy water in her hands and drank.

In this vast, bleak place there was not a sign of life excepting the breath of the wind. She wondered at the bright lights of stars in the lake. Then she saw that they were reflected not only on the water, but on the beach too. Each star in the sky had its double below. She cupped a tiny silver whorl in her hands. Its companion above was so dim it could barely be seen, but she was sure it twinkled as she tucked the stone into her bag. Take a treasure to remember. Wooden footsteps crunched against pebbles. For a moment, the old woman felt glad of the company. She was relieved not to be alone in this big, dark place. Tides of shingle shifted as the small girl thundered towards her, arms outstretched. What did the child want from her? Clutching her bag in her hands, the old woman sprang into the air and ran.

When she'd gone round and round the world and down the street she finally reached the market. It was all very well gallivanting about, she thought, but this was where she'd meant to go.

There were the normal stalls, of knickers and nighties, second hand books, the egg man, fruit and veg, but that afternoon there were also stalls with things she hadn't seen in a long time: Lyons' Cocoa, Fry's chocolate, Vim and Sunlight Soap. At one of these stalls a man was already packing up.

'What's that?' she asked.

'Some old wooden doll. Its feet are half worn away so it won't stand up. I found it just now, at the side of the road.'

'Are you going to sell her?'

'Maybe. Seems a shame to throw her away or to just leave her here.'

'How much?'

'How much do you have?' The man continued to pack things away into boxes.

The woman reached into her bag and discovered she'd forgotten to bring her purse. 'I have the last leaf from the hollow hawthorn in the woods, a white feather from a red rooftop in a city by the sea, and a silver stone that mirrors a star in the sky,' she said, but as she rooted around in her bag her fingers found a hole. The treasures had gone.

The man looked up at her. 'What was that you said, love?'

'It doesn't matter. I wanted to keep them anyway, to remember.'

'Look, if you really want her she's yours. Not much use to me. I'll be packed up soon. Do you need a lift?'

The man was looking at her feet. And she realised

with horror the slippers had gone. She hadn't felt them melt away, but she was standing on the flags in her stockinged feet. Her age wrapped around her in an instant. Every ache locked back into her bones. 'Yes, thank you. A lift would be very nice.'

The wooden girl was an absent companion. She perched on the settee, while the woman sat in her high-backed chair waiting for the girl to move, to do something, but all life seemed to have left her along with her feet.

There were lines on the girl's face, cracks that made an old woman of her. Watching her all afternoon, the woman began to see patterns in the cracks—they were ordered like pieces of a jigsaw. She approached cautiously and ran her fingers over the girl's forehead. Beneath her touch a misshapen drawer emerged and in it there was a leaf. In another she found a white feather, and in another she found a stone.

There were dozens more tiny drawers, like the doors of an Advent calendar. She opened them up one by one and found within each a treasure and its memory: a scrap of bandage from a knee scraped when she was playing chase with Bill Morris; a thre'penny bit given to her by her grandmother on the day she wasn't chosen to be Rose Queen. There were ribbons and shells and fragments of lost letters. And in the heart-drawer of the girl she found May blossom, so fragile and old she was scared to let her breath touch the petals. And she remembered: as a child she had followed the fairy path and played beneath a tree in the woods. She planted any treasures she had between its roots. She'd asked the tree to keep them safe for her always, so she wouldn't lose anything, so she wouldn't forget.

Acknowledgements

A special thank you to John Patrick Pazdziora for his patience, care and incredible commitment to making this book real.

Thank you to Laura Rae for illustrating it so beautifully.

Many thanks to editors, friends and family for all their support over the last few years, especially to Nicholas Royle, Andy Darby, Sarah Hymas, Ra Page, Erzebet Barthold, Defne Çizakça, Michael Kelly, Colin Meldrum, Angela Leroux-Lindsay, Robert Sheppard, Ailsa Cox, Daniele Pantano, Dinesh Allirajah, Elizabeth Burns, Andy Hedgecock, Faye Hanson, Anna McKerrow, Carys Bray, the Edge Hill MA group 2009-11, all at Northern Lines, Lianne Graham, Bernie Snape, Emma Curwood, Diane Gunning, Nicola Preece, Tim Franklin, Jonathan Bean, Maria Major, Angela Diggle, Myriam Frey, Liz Edwards, and Emma and Eamonn Bolger.

With thanks and love always to Lin, Graham and Louise Dean.

SOURCE NOTES
The quotation on p. x is taken from Aragon, L. Translated by Taylor, S.W. (1994) *Paris Peasant*. Boston: Exact Change. The quotation on p. 3 is taken from Grimm, J. & Grimm, W. Translated by Crane, L. (1993) *Grimm's Fairy Tales*. Ware: Wordsworth Editions. The quotation on p. 58 is taken from MacDonald, G. (1858) *Phantastes*. London: Smith, Elder and Co.

Lightning Source UK Ltd.
Milton Keynes UK
UKHW020439290322
400728UK00006B/394